HARRY NAVINSKI

The Test

A Detective Silvester Locke-Croft Murder Mystery

Contents

Foreword

This short story fills in some of DCI Suzanna McLeod's back-story, specifically the test – mentioned in *The Glass* – that she took and passed to gain her inheritance from her great-great-uncle. The setting is 1920s London and the language and style of writing fit that era and situation.

The next book in the Suzanna McLeod series, *The Duty*, moves from Victorian London back to modern-day Edinburgh in 2015. Be prepared for a jump. If you've not read *The Glass*, I recommend you do so before reading *The Duty*, because you'll get to know Suzanna. It's not essential though, because each chapter of her life stands alone.

If you enjoy this story and wish to read more of my work, please follow the link to my website at the end of this book, where, if you haven't already, you can sign up to be notified when I release my next novel. Happy reading...

***

I

Part One

The Instruction

Sometime in the 1930s

(copy of Prologue from 'The Glass')

Beside the Queen Anne style armchair in which the elderly gentleman sat was a crackling open fire, its radiance warming his legs, as it sought to hold off the wintery chill that had blown in when the visitor had entered.

Classical music played quietly on the gramophone behind him. The lens of a magnifying glass glistened with the reflected light of the table lamps, as the man twizzled it between his fingers, feeling the smoothness of its shaft.

The recently polished brass rim glowed with reflected firelight. Its mahogany handle was intricately inset with ivory diamond shapes. But despite having evidently been cherished, the dents in its frame indicated that it had been a working tool, not just an ornament.

He set the object on the side table as he focused on the task. The man's piercing eyes looked upwards as if gazing through the ceiling, seeking guidance from the stars. He had his hands together, prayer-style, the tips touching his prominent chin. He'd led a risky life that included taking cocaine and smoking opium, and he'd been injured many times in his clashes with various criminals. It was amazing that he'd lived into his seventies.

A man was perched on the sofa opposite, his knees held together, and his briefcase laid on his lap, in use as a writing table. Unlike the old man – in his aubergine silk dressing gown – the younger man wore a pinstripe suit and white shirt with a dark nondescript tie. The solicitor awaited instructions.

"As you know," his elderly client said, "I never married, so have no spouse to whom I can leave my assets, and I *certainly* do not wish my brother to inherit my estate. To my knowledge, I did not sire any offspring, but I do have a niece and a nephew. Despite my dislike for my brother, his children never wronged me. I prefer their offspring benefited, rather than the Government that I served throughout the last war. They've already had enough from me."

"My brother's children are middle-aged and possess sufficient wealth, so I am not inclined to make them richer. Even their children are now in adulthood and making their way in life. My legacy, therefore, may go to *their* children."

"Excuse me, sir. Please explain your desires further. It is not yet clear to me who should inherit your wealth?"

"Yes, of course! I had not finished. What I leave behind will go to a descendent of my brother (note the singular, Mr Hicks), who on reaching the age of eighteen meets the conditions that I will set. Each child in my brother's line will be offered the opportunity to take a test, administered by your company. If passed, this person will inherit my entire estate. Do you understand?"

"Yes, sir."

"On my death, all my goods and chattels are to be sold. Proceeds from these sales are to be amalgamated with my investments and bank holdings to form my estate, which is to be placed into a trust fund. The only exception to these instructions is that this magnifying glass must *not* be sold." The old man held it up again for the solicitor to observe.

"It is to be retained in its cloth bag, along with a letter that I will write. Your good company shall keep it safe until an entitled relative successfully analyses the test scenario I will provide. A solution to this mystery will also be supplied for your company to use in judging the submissions. Only when the test is passed shall your company pass the letter and magnifying glass to the successful person, along with the proceeds of the trust fund."

"If any of my brother's offspring fail this test, they will get nothing. If one generation fails, their children are to be given the opportunity, and *their* children, cascading downwards until someone with the right talent, intellect and character solves the case. Have I made myself clear?"

"Yes, sir. I fully understand your instructions. Will the test and letter be ready for me on my return?"

"Yes. Now be off with you and return with the will and trust fund deeds before the end of the week. I do not know how much longer I will live." He picked up his pipe and lit it, retreating into his private thoughts.

The solicitor rose and left as the fragrance of sweet tobacco drifted across to him. He knew from previous sessions with the eccentric old man that he would say no more and expect no goodbyes.

* * *

A Few Days Later

"Come in, Mr Hicks."

Hicks was flabbergasted. How did he know it was him? He hadn't made an appointment. His client never ceased to amaze him.

The solicitor had returned to his client's apartment near Marylebone Station with the trust deed and will. The gentleman's landlady, who lived in the ground floor apartment, had let him in and escorted him upstairs, before knocking on the door.

Hicks entered the apartment and was immediately questioned by the old man.

"Do you have the required documents for my scrutiny?"

Today the gentleman was fully dressed, in his suit with a waistcoat, and his oxblood brogue shoes gleamed.

"Yes, sir. Are the test and letter ready to accompany the will?"

"Of course. Did I not say they would be!"

"My apologies, sir."

"Sit yourself down, Hicks, and pass me the documents."

He did as he was told, and noticed his client feel the quality of the paper, before nodding his approval. His company always used the best paper available: thick, textured and with a tiny hint of amber colour, giving it the look of parchment.

As ever when in the presence of this man, he perched on the front of his seat with his knees clamped together – unable to relax. His client focused on the will and deed, so Hicks just sat glancing around the apartment.

Coal was smouldering in the grate and a troop of brass fire tools stood to attention on the left side, as if waiting to be ordered into action. The fire surround was black cast iron, inlaid with beige and green patterned tiles. On the mantelpiece were a number of objects – not ornaments. A cloth bag, which presumably held the magnifying glass, sat on the corner within reach of his client and next to it was a burr walnut tobacco pipe. Beyond the whiff of burning coal, the aroma of tobacco still hung in the air, accompanied by a faded sweet incense.

Further along the mantle, a small brass bell waited to be used, but Hicks could not think when such an occasion would occur, as the man had no servants. On the left side a pewter flip-lid match case, with inset semi-precious stones, sat open with a dozen or so vestas ready to be struck on the container's serrated base.

On one side of the apartment, bookshelves covered the entire wall, overflowing with books, documents, magazines, and assorted articles. Leaning against these shelves in the corner adjoining the fireplace wall, a well-used violin rested, its bow's broken horsehairs sticking out like cat's whiskers. A white china vase sat on the fireside table, naked without flowers.

Peering through the open bedroom door, Hicks saw a marble-topped mahogany washstand, its bowl, and jug in rose-patterned pink and green. A carved, dark oak headboard acted as a backdrop to the bedcovers that were strewn across the large bed. The window was closed, and he could detect the scent of sweaty sheets.

After some time, the gentleman looked up at the solicitor. "I am impressed with your work, Hicks. My wishes are documented accurately in the will and testament. The trust deed also says exactly as I had directed. Now to the matter of my letter and test."

Hicks smiled at being complimented. It was unusual for this to happen. Perhaps his client was even closer to death's door than he expected and had mellowed in his last days on the earth? Although, he gave no outward sign that he was ill.

"In this sealed envelope is the letter to the person who will inherit my estate. I take it you possess your company's seal, so we can secure the envelope?"

"Yes, sir. It is here," Hicks said, opening his attaché case.

"Good. Then seal it now in my presence. Then you can place it securely in your case. It is important that no one but the recipient, gets sight of what is written in the letter."

Hicks duly melted wax across the envelope flap, its scent swirling into the room, and pressed the company's seal into it until it hardened.

"Excellent. Now, this second envelope contains the test, and the third envelope holds the solution. Combined, they read as a short story based loosely on an investigation in which I assisted the Metropolitan Police. The details, however, have been changed and the consulting detective is a fictional character. The final section of the story concludes the mystery.

To supplement the story, a set of accompanying documents provides supporting evidence to assist them in their assessment. The person taking the test will read the story and scrutinise these appendices, located in envelope 4, before submitting their appraisal of the case. This submission must provide details of the murderer, his or her means, motive, and opportunity.

The flaps of these envelopes are not stuck down, nor shall they be sealed. Your company will undoubtedly require access to their contents a number of times over the years until someone passes the test. They must be kept separate from each other to ensure that no one is accidentally provided with the solution. Do you understand?"

"I completely understand, sir, and will make sure that your directions are carried out."

"I am confident that you will. Here, take them." His client passed him three buff, foolscap envelopes, two of which evidently contained thick wads of papers.

Hicks leaned across the gap and took the envelopes, checking that each was correctly marked *Test Solution* and Appendices, before placing them in his case.

Your will and testament will require two witness signatures. I can act as one of them. Perhaps the lady from downstairs would assist.

The aged gentleman lifted the bell from its resting place and gave it a shake. Two minutes later, the landlady knocked on the door and entered, to Hick's amazement.

"Ah! Mrs Shuttleworth. Would you be so kind as to witness my signature on these documents?"

"Of course."

His client signed the documents, and Mrs Shuttleworth did as she'd been requested, before leaving as quietly as she had arrived, without any thanks. Hicks took the documents, added his signatures, slid them back in their envelopes and placed them into his case. "Will that be all, sir?"

"Yes. I shall have no further need of your services. I am sure you will be notified when I am gone, and the will is to be enacted. Thank you for your professional assistance."

Hicks rose from the chair, bowed, and walked to the door, opening it before stepping onto the threshold. "Sir, may I enquire why you believe you shall not be on this earth for much longer?"

"No, you may not."

Hicks left the apartment without another word. He was keen to read what his client had put into the test as soon as he had some spare time.

* * *

Hicks finished his day at the office and returned to his home, a four-storey Edwardian townhouse in Manchester Square. He loved that there was a private natural space in the centre of the square where occupants of the surrounding properties could relax when the weather was suitable.

Today was not one of those days, as grey clouds hung low over the city and soot emanated from virtually every chimney. He could already taste the coal thickened air. Later this mist and smoke would likely descend fully to the streets, and on these wintery, still days, London's smog would choke their lungs.

He opened his door and called out to his spouse. His children came running and his wife appeared a few seconds later to welcome him home. The aroma of cooking emanated from the kitchen – beef casserole by the smell of it; his stomach rumbled in anticipation.

* * *

After dinner, his stomach now full, Hicks retired to the drawing room, sat on a dark red leather chesterfield sofa, and placed the collection of large buff envelopes on the table in front of him. He rose again and fetched a glass of port to enjoy during his reading time. Normally he would peruse the Daily Telegraph, but this evening he had brought work home. He *could* leave the scrutiny of this work to another day, but he was intrigued by what his client had written and wished to check its legibility.

He picked up the envelopes, selected the one marked *Test*, removed its contents, and began to read.

* * *

II

Part Two

The Test

The Test - Foreword

If you are reading this document, you will have reached your eighteenth birthday and been offered the opportunity to inherit my estate. You may have learned that I passed much of my time on this earth helping the Metropolitan Police to convict criminals. My assistance was normally called upon when the police believed they were up against a master criminal, and they required a superior mind to track them down. Alternatively, my aid was sought when a case had proven to be more complex than they could manage. My involvement was only requested for these extraordinary cases.

I never found a woman to be my bride, nor sired children, so had no one to pass on my moderate wealth when my time came to depart this earth. I wished my residual wealth to pass to someone worthy – someone with a superior mind, perhaps equal to mine – although unlikely.

You shall now read the story, written as a short crime novel. If you are not blessed with a photographic memory and an incredible ability to recall facts, you would do well to take notes. After reading the first section of this novella, you should consider the accompanying reports attached as appendices, which provide further evidence.

There is sufficient information within the story and appendices for you to work out who murdered the victim and why. Your answer must explain your reasoning as well as naming the accused. You should view this as you might an exam in which you are given a complex algebraic question.

If you were to provide an answer with no workings, but made a simple mistake, you would score zero. But if you provided your workings, the examiner would note your mathematical abilities were sound bar the single mistake that led to an erroneous result. In this case, a score of 90% might still be achieved, despite the incorrect figure given as the answer. So too, in the test on which you shall now embark.

After your answer has been assessed, you will be notified of the result. If successful, a copy of the final section of the story, the *Solution*, will be provided to you. This document leads to the unveiling of the criminal, so you may compare it with your own conclusion. If you fail the test, this cannot be revealed to you, because there would be a temptation to tell another person in the chain and thus pervert the entire exercise.

It would be traditional to offer you good luck. But luck is not what is required. Your success or failure stands on your ability to unravel the facts of the crime, analysing the information and reaching the right conclusion. There is no luck involved in such an exercise.

If you pass the test, I wish you well in your life, making the most of what you will inherit. Please take great care of the one article that will pass into your hands and ensure it is handed onto future generations. If you fail, then you are unworthy of further words.

* * *

18th May 1927 – Murder in the Mews

A whistle sounded shrilly in Ulster Place, then a shout sounded, "Hey You. Stop," followed by another whistle blast. PC Richards had heard glass break and had seen a man emerge from Park Square Mews. He gave chase as the man started running up Brunswick Place. On reaching the end, the fugitive swung right, then ran across Ulster Terrace towards the entrance to Regent's Park.

A horse drawing a hansom cab nearly ran into the man, as he hurried across the road, pulling up sharply and throwing the cab's occupant off her seat onto the floor. The horse snorted and pulled back its head. The cab driver barely stayed in *his* seat. He stood and shouted at the maniac as he ran away. Richards took the same route, past the stationary horse, reaching the pavement as his quarry entered through the park gates.

He struggled to keep up with the man, his weighty hobnail boots encumbering his feet, and their soles slipped on the cobbles. He reached the gates just in time to see the man look back before turning right. The PC glimpsed the fugitive's features: a long Roman nose, perched above thin lips. He had a ruddy complexion, and his forehead was shaded by a cloth cap. The PC blew his whistle again and called, "Stop that man!" But no one appeared to have heard. He reluctantly gave up the chase, realising he would never catch him.

As he retraced his route across Ulster Terrace, the stench of fresh equine droppings reminded him of the danger he'd been in when he followed the fugitive past the distressed horse.

* * *

On his return to Park Square Mews, PC Richards noted a man in plain clothes was talking with a gathering of uniformed officers, and they were intent upon his instructions. Twenty minutes had passed since he first sounded the warning, and he assumed they had gathered because of his earlier whistling and shouting.

He grabbed one of his colleagues as they dispersed to go about their duties. "George," he said to his friend from the station. "What's happening?"

"That geezer is Detective Inspector Harrison. He's from Scotland Yard. There's been a murder at Number 7 in the mews. We're to put a cordon around the area while he investigates."

Richards approached Harrison and introduced himself. "Excuse me, sir. Constable Richards at your service. I was here earlier and heard glass breaking. Shortly afterwards, a man ran out from the mews and when I shouted at him, he took off."

"Go on, Richards."

"I blew my whistle numerous times during the chase, but no one helped, and he finally gave me the slip in the park. Is there anything I can do to aid you, sir?"

"Yes. The other PCs will keep the public away. Come with me, Constable. I may need your assistance at the crime scene."

Richards followed the inspector into the mews and noticed glass by the window of Number 7. Inspector Harrison approached the scene gingerly. Glass fragments were inside the house and some had fallen outside.

The sash window was secured in the closed position, and Inspector Harrison turned to the constable. "Richards. Why do you think the culprit smashed the glass to escape, when he could have just opened the window?"

"Er... Perhaps the catch is stuck, sir?"

Harrison reached his left arm through the broken glass and tried the catch, his face showing strain as he attempted to turn it, but without success. "There's our answer then. Well done, Constable." The inspector noted this in his book, before directing Richards towards the door.

On entering the house, a stench like an uncleaned public lavatory hit their senses. The victim's bowl and bladder must have voided after death. Harrison gave no sign that the disgusting odour perturbed him. Richards, however, retched at the stink and struggled to hold down his dinner, as his eyes caught sight of the bloodied body.

The inspector looked around, taking in the room's character, and assessing the likely route of the struggle. A three-column, grey painted iron radiator stood beneath the window. Shards of glass perched on top of the radiator, and some pieces were on the oak-boarded floor at its base. A large rug sat in the centre of the room, rucked up in a wave emanating from where the body laid. Its patterning included various flowers and geometric shapes, and he noted that it had been intricately woven, predominantly with rose red, royal blue, and off-white yarns.

A gloriously shiny walnut writing bureau abutted the wall opposite the window, above which was a mirror with gleaming copper frame. The bureau's writing flap was hanging below horizontal, with the righthand hinge warped and screws pulled away.

19

An easy chair with Queen Anne style legs stood in the corner, its green baize fabric contrasting with the purple walls. It appeared untouched by the struggle. Beside the chair was an occasional table, also in walnut, but its surface was dull and scratched. The table was on its side and a china cup and saucer laid on the rug. A damp patch indicated that the cup had contained liquid when the table had been toppled.

Two feet above the inspector's head, a chandelier of cut-glass pendants hung from a hook in the centre of a moulded plaster rose. The single electric lightbulb that had hung from the twin-flex wires, emanating from the centre of the moulding, was broken. Pieces of thin spherical glass lay scattered on the floor.

The inspector put his left hand to his face, his forefinger covering his upper lip and his thumb touching his cheekbone, giving the impression that he was deep in thought. He noticed movement and turned towards the open door as a middle-aged man entered.

PC Richards didn't recognise this man and was about to challenge him when the inspector greeted him. "Good day, Doctor Williams. Sorry you had to be called out on this damp day, but as you can see, we have a dead body."

The doctor ignored Harrison, placed his leather bag on the floor and knelt beside the cadaver. He tested for a pulse, finding none, then continued his examination of the clammy body.

PC Richards took a step towards the chair and bent down before picking something up from the floor. It was a lapel stud badge with three linked oval rings. He passed it to the inspector, who thanked him and slipped it into his breast pocket, showing no sign of recognition.

"What can you tell me, Doctor?"

"I cannot be certain about the cause of death or exactly when it took place until the autopsy has been completed. But my initial findings suggest the victim died from a cut to the throat and subsequent bleeding. There are signs of a physical conflict, with, as you can see, furniture and articles displaced. There's bruising on the man's arms and neck, confirming there had been a struggle.

The murderer would undoubtedly have had blood on his hands and arms, but might have been relatively clear on the rest of his clothing. The fatal wound will have been inflicted from behind, resulting in the blood gushing away from his assailant."

Harrison turned to Richards, "Constable. Did you notice blood on the person you chased?"

"I can't be certain, sir. The light was dim from the heavy cloud cover and he ran past me at speed."

Just then another man entered, dressed similarly to the inspector, in a formal suit and a Bowler hat. The officer, Goldsworthy, greeted Harrison, who acknowledged his presence by lifting his eyes before re-focussing on his examination of the scene. Richards and Goldsworthy made eye contact and nodded a subdued greeting.

Harrison looked up again and spoke to Richards: "You can return to your duties, Constable Richards now that DC Goldsworthy has arrived. Please write up a report when you finish your duty on the beat."

"Yes, sir. Will do. Good luck with finding the culprit." He nodded to the DC, turned, and left the building.

* * *

"Right Goldsworthy, look around the rest of the house and note everything you observe, while I continue to ponder the crime scene."

"Yes, sir." Goldsworthy wandered off, first entering the kitchen. He noticed a knife block stood next to the range cooker, with one knife missing. He searched around the room but didn't find it. If the missing implement was the murder weapon, the assailant must have been in this room before carrying out the deed. There was no knife in the reception room where the body laid, so it must be somewhere else in the house or have been taken away by the murderer.

There was no sign of a struggle and nothing else came to his attention, so he moved on. In the dining room a large mirror sat above the fireplace, its carved mid-brown oak frame hinting at a French connection. The wood of the large table matched the mirror. He'd noticed this latest trend in several homes owned by the wealthier, well-travelled individuals. It would seem that mahogany was becoming old-fashioned. But he was surprised to see these pieces here, given the modesty of the home.

On the floor was a green and beige patterned rug, which partly covered the parquet flooring. Eight matching chairs surrounded the table, with the end chairs having arms, affording higher status to the men who usually occupied them on formal occasions – like kings, sat on their thrones.

Two cupboards sandwiched a set of drawers in the sideboard, the shallower drawer at the top and the deeper at the bottom. Again, the wood matched the other furniture. It was carved in the same style, with swirls and interconnecting leaves, as if a long wreath. He looked closely at the sideboard and noticed that a fine layer of dust covered most of it, but there were two circular dust-free shapes at either end.

He returned to the sitting room, where the inspector was still pondering. "Sir," he said, catching his boss's attention,

"There's a knife missing from the kitchen and I've found an anomaly in the dining room."

"And?"

"Going by the dust patterns on the top surface of the sideboard, a pair of candelabra were recently removed."

"Aha, that would explain it. The chap that PC Richards chased had probably taken the candelabra – no doubt made from silver – and was caught in the act by the owner. A fight took place and after murdering Finchley, the thief made his escape through the broken window. We must focus on finding the intruder."

Goldsworthy looked surprised. His boss had already identified the victim, rapidly concluded the motive, and identified the likely culprit. Tracking down the attacker who'd escaped wouldn't be easy, though. "Right then, I'd better speak with the neighbours and find out if anyone can identify the intruder."

The inspector agreed.

* * *

After Goldsworthy left the house, Harrison checked that the pathologist was still examining the body, then looked around upstairs. There were two bedrooms and a bathroom. One bedroom had a single bed, covered with a white counterpane. There was also a mahogany wardrobe, and a damask-covered bedside table, on which stood a lamp. It looked undisturbed, so he moved into the second bedroom.

This must be where the occupant slept. It was larger and had a three-quarter bed and a double wardrobe. On the dressing table, a perfume bottle, and a woman's hairbrush filled the otherwise devoid space. He examined the bottle and smelled the perfume. Very pleasant. No doubt expensive.

The inspector opened the wardrobe and peered inside. A woman's dressing gown hung separately from the other clothes, confirming his suspicion that the man had a lover. Men's suits, trousers, and white shirts filled the rest of the wardrobe, and on the base laid a cardboard box.

He removed the box and laid it on the bed, then lifted its lid and delved inside. He extracted a pile of documents and leafed through them until he came to the man's birth certificate – it would be required to prove his identity. Reading the details confirmed the victim's name. James Reginald Finchley, born 22nd July 1898. Place of Birth: Denham. Father: Herbert Charles Finchley. Mother: Amelia Rosemary Finchley.

Harrison recognised the father's name. He was now *Lord* Herbert Finchley. The peer had a large house in Mayfair and an estate in Buckinghamshire. It surprised him that James didn't live in a larger house, given his father's wealth.

He dug deeper into the documents and found a certificate from the Law Society confirming James Finchley's membership, and another paper awarding his degree in law. A pay receipt showed that he worked at Chippenham and Dudley Solicitors, of Weymouth Street – just a short walk from the man's home. Harrison put these aside and scanned through the remaining documents before placing them back in their box.

He checked the bathroom before heading downstairs, finding nothing of importance.

* * *

As Harrison reached the bottom step, another man entered the house carrying bulky equipment. "Ah, Penfold, good that you got here in reasonable time. The body's through in that room.

Doctor Williams will shortly complete his work, so you'll be able to start your work soon."

The photographer acknowledged the inspector's remarks and walked through to where the body lay. The doctor was packing away his instruments as Penfold entered. "Good day to you, doctor. Have you finished your work?"

Williams looked round, his face as deadpan as the corpse's. "Yes. I'll leave you to it. Please deliver a set of photographs to me at the mortuary once you've developed them."

"Of course, doctor. I'll waste no time getting them to you, and a set for Inspector Harrison."

Doctor Williams checked around to make sure he'd repacked everything into his bag, then walked out of the house without another word.

Harrison completed his appraisal of the crime scene, then left Penfold to his work, leaving the property by the front door, and went in search of his DC.

* * *

Harrison strolled along the mews looking for signs of the detective constable and spotted him near the end of the cul-de-sac. On reaching his subordinate, he stood and waited for him. Goldsworthy turned away from the person he'd been speaking to and joined his boss, ensuring the man had closed his door before speaking.

"I've knocked on thirteen doors but only found four people at home. None of whom noted any unusual activity today."

The inspector didn't seem surprised. In fact, he looked content. "Please complete your work, Goldsworthy. I shall return to the Yard and write up my report. I expect you to submit yours to me by the end of your shift. The DCI will require an update before we call it a day."

"Yes, sir. I don't expect I will be too long, going by what I've found so far. It's surprising how little people notice about what happens on their street."

"That's human nature, Constable. They're busy living their own lives and rarely observe what goes on around them unless it directly affects them... I'll see you later." He turned and strode away, leaving the DC to his duties.

Goldsworthy knocked on the next door and stood waiting for an answer, wondering if he would find anyone who'd seen something. It was three door-knocks later that his luck changed.

An elderly lady opened the door at Number 2. She was dressed in an ankle length plain, dark dress with a full skirt and puffed shoulders. She had a lacy bonnet perched on her short, curly grey hair.

"Good day, ma'am. Detective Constable Goldsworthy, Metropolitan Police."

Above her petite nose, the old lady's eyebrows rose, but she waited for him to continue.

"There's been a crime committed just down the street from you. Have you noticed any unusual occurrences in the last two hours?"

"What crime has been committed, Constable?"

"A murder, ma'am, and we need to find the culprit and bring him to justice."

The lady looked shocked at the news. "Oh dear! How dreadful."

"Have you seen anything of note?"

"There was a shout. It must have been about an hour ago, now – perhaps a little more. I was just having a cup of tea when I

26

heard it. I almost spilled my drink, and my biscuit fell from the saucer onto the floor. It broke and sent crumbs all over the rug."

The lady's frilly necked dress was evidently tickling her chin, as she placed her finger in the frill and slid it round the front to pull it away from her skin.

Goldsworthy jotted down details in his notebook. "Did you *see* anything, as well as hearing the shout?"

"Yes. I moved to my window and noticed a man run past, towards Marylebone Road."

"What can you tell me about the man?"

"He wore a flat cap and a brown tweed jacket. His trousers were dark, but I couldn't tell you what colour they were."

"And his height and build?"

"Let me think... He was medium height – difficult to say exactly with no comparison and such little time to see him."

"Of course, ma'am. I understand. And his build?"

"Skinny, I would say – certainly not fat. More like a whippet than a bulldog."

"Do you recall anything about his features?"

"He ran past at speed, so I didn't see much, but I did notice he had a long aquiline nose. There's nothing else I can tell you, I'm afraid. If that's all, I'd like to get back inside, as I'm getting chilled. When you get to my age, you feel the cold more than when you're young."

"Certainly, ma'am. I just need to record your name, for my report."

"It's Miss Maplethorpe, Elise. I never married. I passed up my one opportunity to wed when I was in my twenties. I wasn't sure if I loved George and couldn't say yes to his proposal. That was a mistake. He soon moved on–"

"Thank you for helping me, Miss Mablethorpe. Most helpful,"

Goldsworthy said, interrupting her romantic reminiscences.

"It's *Maple*thorpe, Constable, not *Mable*thorpe."

"Sorry, ma'am. Maplethorpe," he said, correcting his note-book entry. "Hopefully, we'll not need to trouble you again." He walked away, knocked on the next door and stood back, waiting for an answer.

No other neighbours answered their doors that day, so Goldsworthy set off to Scotland Yard to brief the DI on his findings and write up his report.

* * *

"Thanks for the briefing, Goldsworthy. Let me have your written report, soonest. Details of the running man correlate with PC Richards' account of the man he chased. Problem is, there will be thousands of men in London meeting that scant description. Best you get knocking on doors along Brunswick Place, tomorrow. And try to find a hansom cab driver who's heard about the Ulster Terrace incident. It shouldn't be difficult – there's so few hansom cabs left in London, nowadays."

"Will do, sir." He turned and strode off to track down Richards and to write his report. More legwork would be required tomorrow.

* * *

19th May

Harrison strode along the corridor towards PC Richards. The inspector was wearing a pristine coat, the sleeves of which reached tidily to his wrists, as they should. He looked very smart. "Thanks for your assistance yesterday, Richards, and your report. The chief inspector will be impressed with your work."

Richards remembered that when he'd last seen Harrison at the house in Park Square Mews, his sleeves were short and the fit of the coat too tight. "Thank you, sir," he said, looking up at the inspector. "I hope you're making good progress on catching the murderer?"

"Don't worry yourself about that, Constable. We'll get the culprit. Be sure of it. You just stay vigilant when patrolling our streets."

Harrison marched off, without waiting for a response, and Richards watched him walk away. He found it difficult to respect the officer; he was so arrogant.

Before Richards reached the locker-room, Goldsworthy emerged from one of the other offices. "Ah! Ernest. Where are you heading today?"

"Hello Cuthbert. I'm on the same patch as yesterday – around the south side of Regent's Park. Why do you ask?"

"I must make enquiries on the route you took when chasing the suspect and wondered whether you could help me?"

"I can show you the route I took if that would help, and I should be able to knock on a few doors for you."

"Excellent. Good man. Are you ready to head out?"

"I just need to grab my truncheon and whistle from my locker. I'll be with you in a jiffy."

* * *

The two constables walked together towards Regent's Park. Today was clearer. There was a breeze and sunshine, but it was still chilly. "So, how's the detective life for you, Cuthbert? Are you glad you transferred?"

"It's better than burning shoe leather eight hours a day. I was so tired when I finished work, I used to fall asleep in my chair after dinner. My relationship with Mabel suffered because we rarely had time to talk about life and our futures. I didn't even have enough energy to put my little one to bed. Now I'm not on my feet *all* day, I get to read her a story most nights."

"I know what you mean about being tired after a full shift. But you often need to work overtime, when there's a serious case to progress, don't you?"

"Yeah, but that's not every day, and I earn extra cash when that happens, so I can treat Mabel when I get a day off work."

"I expect you'll have been working late this week, with this murder case?"

"As it happens, I've not done any overtime."

"That's unusual. I'm surprised the bosses aren't pushing for a result."

"This is just one amongst many murders in the city, so the

case is likely lost in the fog of multiple crimes. Mind you, if we don't make progress soon, I reckon we'll get pressure from upstairs."

"What do you think about this murder – you know, what the motive was? Who the murderer might be?"

"The DI doesn't like me talking about our case to others. But, because you're a mate, as long as you keep it to yourself, I'm happy to discuss it?"

"Of course, Cuthbert. You can trust *me*."

"I had a good look around the lower floor and noticed that although it's a small property, it's been furnished with new imported carved pieces, from France, I believe. That can't have been cheap. He's a lowly solicitor, so not a wealthy man yet. The furniture seems out of place."

"But his father's Lord Finchley, isn't he?"

"I didn't know. Harrison didn't say when I mentioned the expensive furniture. He appears to be keeping stuff to himself more than usual this time. He's never particularly forthcoming with information about the case he's working. I think he sees knowledge as power. If he's the only one with all the information, he'll be the one who can solve it. He's ambitious."

Richards nodded and pursed his lips, as he thought about what his friend had just said. "What else did you notice about the murder scene?"

"The broken glass pattern is odd. If the murderer had smashed the pane outwards, I'd expect most glass to fall outside, although of course some *would* fall into the house. But it seemed to be the other way around." He paused for a minute, then continued. "Maybe the intruder broke the window to enter the house, to steal the silverware. But James Finchley disturbed him during his burglary and in the ensuing struggle the thief killed him?"

"But that can't be the case, because I heard the glass break, then saw the man running away and gave chase. There wasn't a gap of minutes between the breaking glass and the escape."

"Hmm..." As he went to speak, he stepped into the road, lost in his thoughts. A car rushed past.

"Oi! Watch out!" Richards grabbed at his friend and just saved him from being hit by the vehicle. He smarted from the pain in his wrenched fingernails, pulled back when grabbing his friend's collar.

"Bloody hell, where did that come from? I didn't notice it," Goldsworthy exclaimed. The stench of burnt oil from the car's internal combustion engine, caught in his nostrils, causing his nose to twitch.

"It was travelling far too fast. The Government should put speed restrictions on these narrow streets, so we can stop these mad car drivers risking lives." Richards nursed his tender fingers. "I can always hear a hansom cab heading towards me, because the horses' shoes and hard wheels clatter on the cobbles. But these motorcars, with their rubber tyres, are much quieter.

Goldsworthy looked upset and stood for a minute recovering from the shock of the near miss. "You're right, Ernest. Why don't you suggest it to the chief constable? He has the ear of the Commissioner, who in turn, gets to speak to ministers."

"Good idea. In fact, I heard the Government is drafting a Road Traffic Act, so now would be a good time."

They crossed the cobbled road and continued on their way, carefully looking out for approaching vehicles. They walked up Harley Street, with its Edwardian, five-storey town houses. Railings provided barriers to keep pedestrians from falling into basement stairwells. The lower levels were grand, with high ceilings, large entrance doors and smooth faced stonework. But above that level, many of the properties had plain brickwork. The higher the floor, the lower the ceiling height and the smaller the windows. Richards guessed that, to be a servant in these houses, you would need to be short or watch your head whenever in the servant-level on the top floor.

The constables stopped at No 7 Park Square Mews, which was still cordoned off – a colleague outside, standing guard. They retraced their steps to the junction with Brunswick Place, where Richards had reported first sighting of the running fugitive.

"He came out of the mews at a sprint and turned north. I'd just heard the glass break, so I challenged him to stop and when he ignored me, I blew my whistle and gave chase."

They walked up Brunswick Place, turned right at the end onto Ulster Terrace, then crossed the road and entered the park, just as Richards had done during the pursuit.

"Right, then Ernest. Let's walk back the way we came and knock on some doors. You take one side of the street; I'll take the other. We can meet up again at the lower end of Brunswick Place."

"Sounds like a plan, Cuthbert."

Richards was progressing along the street faster than expected, as the servants answering the doors had all reportedly seen nothing. He crossed the street and started working his way back up Brunswick Place until he met up with Goldsworthy. "How'd it go, Cuthbert?"

"Of all the doors I knocked on, only one reported they'd seen something. How about you?"

"Nothing at all. But if the house owners had seen anything, I'll never know because the servants refused to trouble their masters or mistresses."

33

"Yeah. I had a similar response. The one who was helpful though, remembers seeing the man running up the street, chased by a uniformed police officer. She got a reasonable look at him."

"Oh good! How did she describe him?"

"He was skinny, with a gaunt face and a long nose with a bend half-way down it. I suggested Roman nose, but she didn't know what I was talking about. But it sounded like the man *you* described. Better still, she thought she'd seen him before."

"Did she say where that was?"

"Yeah. The market in Camden Town. Look, I know that's not on your beat, so I'd best let you get back to your duties and take a walk there myself."

"Yeah, you're right. I don't think the sergeant would be happy if he found I was outside my area, especially if a crime happened and I wasn't around to deal with it."

"Thanks for your help, Ernest. I'll let you know how I get on in Camden next time I see you."

"Cheers, Cuthbert. Good luck with your enquiries. See you later."

Goldsworthy strode off towards Camden. He would ask around but wasn't confident of finding the suspect. He didn't possess a photograph or even an artist's impression. In any case, unless they knew the man to be a bad-un, disliked by the community, they'd be unlikely to give him up. He could but try, though.

* * *

20th May

"Have you tracked down that hansom cab driver yet, Constable?" Inspector Harrison asked, after Goldsworthy had entered his office.

"Not yet, sir. But I spoke with a cab driver who knew about the incident. Did you know there's only twelve hansom cabs operating nowadays? The Austin cab has taken over almost completely, so there's a tiny community of hansom drivers. He gave me a name of the driver involved. Would you like me to focus on that today?"

"Yes, you do that. Report back by the end of the day, or earlier if you've completed that task."

Goldsworthy headed out into the fresh late spring air. The sun was shining again. The night had been cool, but the sun's warmth was pleasant. He smiled, glad to be outside instead of sat indoors writing reports.

* * *

"So the man ran across the road in front of your horse, causing you and the passenger to be thrown out of your seats?"

"Yeah, guv. That's right. I thought he could have represented Britain in the Olympics – ran with the speed of a greyhound, he did."

The bench on which he was sat, beside a painted wooden building in the middle of the road, looked uncomfortable. But it was probably no worse than a hansom cab driver's seat.

"What can you tell me about him?"

"Not much, I'm afraid. Had a flat cap on and brown clothes, but I never saw his face. That's all I can tell you."

"Where did the man run after his encounter with your horse?"

The cabby sat his tin mug on the bench and rose quickly. "Oi! You boys clear off. Get away from me 'orse." The horse deposited fresh manure onto the cobbles, as if offering a further incentive for the boys to move on.

After the cabby sat again, Goldsworthy repeated the question, as the dung's pong reached him, causing an involuntary nose spasm.

"Went into the park, he did. Don't know where he went afterwards. I was too busy sorting out me passenger and me 'orse."

"Okay. Thanks for your time, Mr Prentice. I'll let you get back to your work."

"Yeah. Thanks. But there ain't much work for me nowadays. Those bloody Austin cabs have taken all the business. No one seems to want to ride in a hansom cab now. Too slow and difficult to get into, they tell me when I offer them a ride."

"Why don't you retire the horse and get a motorised cab, then?"

The cab driver finished his tea before answering. "I've been doin' this job for thirty years now. Too *old* to change. Don't reckon I could 'andle one of those new cabs, anyway. I'd probably crash it. I'll just struggle on while I can."

* * *

Goldsworthy returned to Scotland Yard to report his findings. "Ah. There you are, sir."

"Yes, Goldsworthy. Here I am. How observant of you," he said sarcastically.

Goldsworthy ignored his boss's response. "I've just got back from interviewing the hansom cab driver. It took ages to find him."

"And?"

"A bit of a waste of time, I'm afraid. He confirmed the incident but didn't see the man's face. What he was able to tell me concurred with other descriptions of the suspect's clothing, and his athleticism. That's about it."

"Okay. Next, I want you to visit Finchley's workplace and see what you can find out about the victim. After that, follow up on the stolen candelabra. Try to find someone who'd been to the house and could describe them. Then check with pawn shops in the area, to ascertain whether anyone has tried to sell a pair recently."

"Right-o, sir. Will do."

* * *

Goldsworthy entered the reception at Chippenham and Dudley Solicitors and spoke with the clerk behind the counter, explaining that Mr Finchley had met his death. The employee almost fainted at the news. He recovered from the shock and informed the firm's partners. They all gathered in the reception. Goldsworthy asked what they knew of Finchley beyond the office and questioned whether anyone had been to his home. None offered any information of use, so he left deflated – another dead end.

* * *

Harrison arrived by cab at the home in Grosvenor Square. Like many of the six-storey homes in Mayfair, surrounding their private parkland, it was a grand affair. Its ground floor stonework was substantial, with building blocks the size of short coffins. The doorway was wide, and the lintel bowed like a small colourless rainbow.

He pressed the bellpush. As it sounded, his heartbeat rose in anticipation of his meet with Lord and Lady Finchley. People born into wealth and privilege would look down on him, and he felt akin to a child waiting outside his headmaster's office.

The butler opened the door. "Inspector Harrison, I presume?" The chief constable had already primed the Finchleys.

Harrison nodded his head and showed his police badge.

"Come this way, sir."

He stepped into a spacious entrance hall, where the butler offered to take his coat. Normally, he would not have agreed to the offer, but the house was too warm to wear an overcoat.

Having taken his coat, the butler showed him into the drawing room and offered a seat and tea, which he accepted. The tea arrived before the Finchleys. He assumed they were too important to drop whatever they were doing to aid the police, even though their own son's murder was under investigation.

When they entered the room, Harrison stood. "DI Harrison. How do you do?" He offered his hand, but neither moved to shake it.

They stood straight and Lord Finchley addressed the inspector.

"What can we do for you, Harrison?"

"Sir," he responded, looking into the Lord's eyes, "I have some questions to ask regarding your son."

"Of course, Inspector. Ask away. Waste no more time."

"We noticed that there appeared to be a pair of candelabra missing from your son's house. They would have been on the dining room sideboard. Did you perhaps see such items when visiting your son, and could you describe them?"

"We've only been to the house once, about three months ago. I certainly didn't see any." He turned to his wife. "Did *you* notice any?"

"Absolutely not."

"What can you tell me about his social life, friends, acquaintances, lovers?"

Lord Finchley spoke for them both. "We do not know what he did with himself. We only see him when he comes to dinner or spends time with us in our country home."

"So you've no idea who might have wished him ill?"

"No. He always got on swimmingly with everyone."

"Sorry to have troubled you, sir. I'll be on my way, then."

"Is that it? You've come all this way for nothing? Where are you with the investigation? Don't you have a suspect?"

"I was hoping you might help me identify other suspects. The only one we have, seems to have disappeared."

Lord Finchley looked peeved. "I expect results soon, Inspector. You'd better be on your way."

* * *

Goldsworthy called the inspector by telephone and reported his lack of progress. Harrison told him that the Finchleys hadn't been able to help with a description of the candelabra but instructed him to check with pawn shops, anyway.

He trudged the streets around Camden enquiring whether anyone had offered to sell the shopkeepers candelabra. But the response was identical at each pawn shop: pursed lips, a tilt of the head, as the shopkeeper thought, then a headshake indicating a negative to his question. He wasn't certain but thought all their responses had been genuine. 'Where next?' he wondered.

On his way back to Scotland Yard, a newsboy distracted him, shouting, "read all about it. Read all about it. Britain signs Treaty of Jeddah. Kingdom of Saudi Arabia born."

He'd been just eighteen when the 1914-18 war had finished. Unlike many of his older colleagues, he'd not travelled outside Great Britain. He was wondering where Saudi Arabia was, as he stepped into the road, and almost walked into the side of a passing cab. Goldsworthy shook himself. That was *twice* in *two days* he'd nearly met with an accident. He resolved to be more attentive in the future.

Keen to get home to his family, when he arrived at the Yard, he eagerly searched for Inspector Harrison, and briefed him on his findings. Harrison listened to Goldsworthy's report, then mentioned how his visit to Lord and Lady Finchley had been a complete waste of time. They knew nothing of his social life and had only visited his mews home once, over three months ago. "You may as well get off home for the weekend, Goldsworthy. I've no idea where to go next with this one."

Goldsworthy *had* some ideas but knew there was little point offering them to his boss.

* * *

23rd May

"George. I'm unhappy with the lack of movement in this Park Square Mews murder case." After a week of little progress in the case, the chief constable had called Superintendent Bateman in for a chat. "Lord Finchley has been onto me about it. Harrison has an excellent reputation for speedily tracking down criminals, but he seems to be dragging his heels on this one."

"Perhaps he's distracted by something. I'll check his workload. He might be handling too many cases?"

"I've already checked and decided action is needed to get things moving again. The department is operating at capacity and, from what I've seen, has no scope for shedding cases or shifting workloads. So I've asked a consulting detective to help us with this. I've used him before — not that you'll be aware of it because the last time I utilised his services, was before you joined the Met."

Bateman sat quietly, pondering his boss's action, and wondering why he'd not spoken with him before inviting a civilian to assist. There was a knock at the door. "Come," the chief constable called out.

A constable opened the door. "I have a visitor for you, sir. A Mr Locke-Croft. I believe you are expecting him."

"Indeed. Show him in, Constable, then return to your duties."

The constable stepped aside, and the visitor entered. He wore a three-piece, herringbone brown tweed suit, a cream shirt, and oxblood brogues. He removed his cloth cap as he entered and laid it on a spare chair. The strong colours of his maroon patterned bowtie drew their eyes to its contrasting status.

"Chief Constable Bookman. Good to see you again, Charles. And this must be Superintendent Bateman," he said, turning to face the other uniformed officer.

Charles had intended to introduce the other two men, but as usual, Silvester Locke-Croft was ahead of him, armed with knowledge and insight beyond his outwardly unintellectual bearing.

"I understand you have a case for me to investigate."

"Yes. Yes. Please sit down, Silvester."

He sat in the offered chair, crossing his left leg over his right, and observed both officers of the law.

"You may be aware, Silvester, of the death of Mr James Finchley-"

"Ah yes, of Park Square Mews."

"Indeed. He's-"

"The son of Lord Herbert Finchley."

"Yes. He's been working-"

"As a solicitor, within the partnership of Chippenham and Dudley, I believe."

The chief constable looked flustered by Locke-Croft's continual interruptions to his briefing. Lines formed on George Bateman's brow and around his eyes and lips, as his face contracted toward his nose. His facial extortions gave away the deepness of his thoughts – trying to assess the stranger before him.

"I understand that Finchley's throat was cut in his own home.

The only sign of potential forced entry being a broken window. But this window was not the murderer's entrance. There was no soil on the carpet, yet outside it was muddy. Furthermore, the evidence indicates Finchley turned away from his enemy before the attack. This suggests the dead man knew his assailant."

"How do you know this Locke-Croft?" The Superintendent asked.

"I called in at the property for a cursory look, on my way to Scotland Yard. The officer on duty was easily persuaded to allow my scrutiny of the scene."

Locke-Croft noticed Bateman jotting in his book, undoubtedly, to remind himself to chastise the constable on duty at the house.

"But how did you know this was the case I wished you to help with?" Charles responded.

"I was aware of the murder and it was obvious to me that he was the son of Lord Finchley. Since there had been no arrests announced, a deduced that you were under pressure from the Lord and required my assistance. Park Square Mews were more or less on my way from my home to Scotland Yard, so I diverted my route to take a cursory look at the scene."

Both officers were astounded.

"I will need sight of all records and reports made so far and will require access to the notebooks of each officer involved in the crime, along with sight of the physical evidence gathered. Furthermore, if I am to identify the culprit, I shall need your authority to interview all officers, plus any witnesses or suspects."

"Of course. I will assign a constable to accompany you and open all such doors. George, please organise this support."

"Superintendent, please arrange for him to be sent to my apartment at 10am in the morning. One more thing, he must be from out with Scotland Yard."

Bateman nodded but said nothing.

Locke-Croft took away the evidence provided to him and returned to his home.

* * *

24th May

"Some rules, Smith," Locke-Croft commanded, with no niceties. The constable assigned to assist the investigation had just arrived and been shown into his apartment. "You may not ask questions, nor take notes. You will not query the actions I take nor the things I say. You are not to report to your colleagues or superiors anything that is said or done."

Smith nodded.

"When I am silent, you shall wait quietly while my mind considers facts. And you will not allow your instincts to break this discipline, by filling these gaps in action or discussion. Your role is merely to accompany me and provide His Majesty's authority as an officer of the law, so I may conduct this investigation. Do you understand?" Locke-Croft said, staring into Smith's eyes.

"Yes, sir."

"Very well. Provided you abide by these rules, I will tolerate you." He turned his back on the constable and continued to study the reports, assigning to memory every little detail that might be important. Two hours passed before he was ready to rise and take the next step. It was now just gone noon.

"Right, Smith. Don your coat. We're going out."

* * *

They took the Underground Metropolitan Line to Euston, then the Hampstead and Highgate Line north to Camden Town, arriving at Inverness Street Market about 2pm. The best fruit and veg had already been sold, but there was still plenty of choice had they been looking to stock up on fresh food. Locke-Croft was shopping for information, though, not edibles.

The plain-clothed policeman tagged along, as the detective wandered around the market handling fruit and chatting to stallholders. When he reached a stall selling beetroot, he picked a bunch and handed it to the man behind the table. "I'll take these, Mr Evans."

Evans took the offered veg and placed them in a brown paper bag before resting them on his balance scales and adding weights to work out how much to charge. "It's good to see you, Mr Locke-Croft. It's been a while. What can I do for you?"

"Indeed, it has, Mr Evans. As ever, I'm in need of your intimate knowledge of the residents of Camden. I must speak urgently with a man about some business in which I'm engaged. He is of medium height, small build and caries no fat. I'm told he runs like a whippet."

Evans's eyes brightened. He already had an idea of who the person might be and envisaged a reward coming his way.

"The fellow is gaunt, has a long Roman nose, a ruddy complexion, thin lips, and has a tendency to wear a cloth cap."

"I think I can help you, sir. Would it be the usual fee?"

"Indeed, Evans. Please tell me his name and where I may find him."

Evans informed Locke-Croft, who committed the information to memory, before passing over extra money, as he paid for the beetroot. "Here. Make yourself useful, Smith. Carry this," he said, passing the beets to the constable, arm outstretched as if the root vegetable smelled terribly.

Smith took the bag without question, then followed Locke-Croft as the detective lengthened his stride, heading west along Inverness Street. He strode along the road until it met Gloucester Crescent, turned right and continued into Oval Road. On reaching James Road Smith looked to the right, noticing that the houses were smaller along that street and had fewer grand architectural features. The Stanhope Arms sat at the corner. They crossed the street and walked along Oval Road, past the Gilbey's Gin Distillery, towards the canal and the goods depot, which served the London Midland and Scottish Railway.

Multiple horse-drawn carts, laden with sacks of flour and other goods, trundled along the road, on their way to markets and wholesalers around London. They entered the depot and Locke-Croft slowed his pace, observing the activity.

He spotted something to his right and swiftly moved until he stood behind a man checking off loads on his clipboard. "Excuse me, Mr Herring. I need a moment of your time."

The man turned, his red face and aquiline nose matching his description. He spotted the constable stood behind Locke-Croft and his muscles tensed, like a sprinter on the blocks. "No need to worry yourself, Mr Herring. I'm not a policeman, although I must admit my assistant looks like one. I'm a private investigator. There are a few questions I must ask you. It won't take long."

The man relaxed a little but was still furtive. His eyes suspiciously returned to Smith, and he continued looking around for signs of other policemen. "I'm a busy man, as you can see. I don't 'ave time for your questions." He turned away again, as if to show they were out of his mind.

"I repeat, sir. This will only take a minute. If you cooperate, I shall not inform the police where they can find you."

Herring reluctantly gave in to Locke-Croft's insistence. "Very well, but only for one minute, or I'll be in trouble with me gaffer. We've got a whole goods train to unload within the next two hours. What is it you want to ask?"

"At approximately 1pm on the eighteenth of May, you were seen running from Park Square Mews. A police officer called for you to stop, then blew his whistle and gave chase. He pursued you up Brunswick Place, along Ulster Terrace, then into Regent's Park, after which he lost sight of you. I just need to know *why* you were running and why you didn't stop when called upon to do so?"

Locke-Croft noted that Herring was considering a denial. He judged the man to be intelligent, if uneducated, so expected him to see sense. He was right.

"Okay. I *was* in that area last week. I'd been on deliveries and the cart had driven off, leaving me to return on foot to Camden, so I started running. They pay me piece-rates when unloading or deliverin'. Anyway, I trotted out of the mews onto Brunswick Place and heard glass break just after I'd run past one of the 'ouses. Next thing I knew, this copper shouted stop and blew his whistle. I was off like a shot. There was no way I was going to get arrested for somethin' I hadn't done and waste days in police custody. I needed to be earning. I've got four 'ungry kids at home and a pregnant wife to feed."

"When did you realise that the policeman had stopped chasing you?"

"I ran across the road – nearly got knocked down by a hansom cab – and ran into the park. I looked back and noticed the policeman just outside the gates. He'd stopped running, was doubled over, and looked like he was gasping for breath. He was obviously not as fit as me. I ran on, keepin' an eye out for him, but he'd stopped following me."

"I see. When you ran along the mews, was there anyone else around who could have broken the window after you passed by?"

"I wasn't paying much attention to things, guv. But I did catch sight of someone in the shadows. Never saw his face though."

"What about his attire? Did you notice anything about how he was dressed?"

"Erm... He had dark clothes on. Smartly dressed, I'd say – not like me. But can't say more than that."

"What about a hat?"

"Not sure. It weren't no cloth cap. Something black and tall. Maybe a rim on it. Look, I really need to get back to work, or the gaffer will sack me for slackin', and I'll be back on loadin' again tomorrow, instead of supervisin'."

"Thank you for your time, and observations, Mr Herring. Your account is perfectly plausible. I shall trouble you no further." He turned and walked away, heading back along Oval Road towards Regent's Park, with Smith in tow.

* * *

Thirty minutes after leaving the rail goods depot, Locke-Croft arrived at Park Square Mews for his second look at the crime scene. He examined the broken pane and footprints in the soil, noting the size and tread and what print laid below the uppermost imprints.

He was astounded to find a coat hanging in the cloakroom with blood on its left sleeve. How could they have missed this? "Smith. Turn around. You're about the same size as the murdered man. I need to assess whether this coat would fit you."

Smith did as he was told, and Locke-Croft laid the coat upon his shoulders, examining the sleeve and body length against his organic model. He noted his finding in his book, then returned it to its peg. "Smith. Note where this coat had been hanging."

Locke-Croft moved into the kitchen and scrutinised the knives in the wooden block sat by the range cooker. The missing knife would have been a suitable weapon for throat cutting.

"Smith. I have another job for you."

"What would you like me to do, sir?"

"Not *like*, Smith; *require*! See these knives. They are all the same design. One is missing. The largest knife has a blade of roughly six inches. The next one in the block is four inches so one can assume the missing knife, which would have sat between, to have a five-inch blade. You must organise a search of the drains along the mews and any other hiding place to find this knife."

"Right, sir. I'll call for extra manpower. It might take a while."

"Nonsense. You can conduct the search, along with the PC on the door. Be assured, no one will come into this house without *my* knowledge."

Smith paused before responding, his lips squeezing together and his upper lip wrinkling. "It shall be done, sir." He walked outside and recruited the duty PC's assistance.

Locke-Croft continued into the dining room, where he examined the furniture. The intricate rose carvings on the chair backs had been skilfully created. The turned front legs had vertical ridges around their circumference, with the shape tapering at top and bottom. They looked slender but solid. He admired the cloth panelled chair backs with matching seat cushions. They should be comfortable. As had been mentioned, the quality of this imported French Art Nouveau dining suite would be more than the wallet of a junior solicitor could manage. But his parents would hardly notice the cost.

The sideboard matched the oak of the table, the rectangular panels creating a reflective pattern. Dust layered the furniture, confirming it was rarely used. He lifted each of the ornaments and noted the gleaming, dust-free surface below. Two circles of exposed lacquer suggested that a pair of candelabra would have adorned this piece. He looked closely at the marks, using his magnifying glass, then noted his findings.

The marks had not been created by lifting round articles from the dust, but by creation of circles within the dust. They were roughly circular but had been made freehand. There were smears from fingers on the shiny surface. He noticed the detail of a fingertip where the anti-clockwise circling had finished.

Locke-Croft moved into the sitting room – the scene of the murder. Dark stains were evident in the floorboards and the rug where the body had lain, its life-giving blood pouring from the gaping throat wound. He observed the patterning and splashes on walls and furnishings.

There were marks on the wooden floor, where the rug had shifted, so he knelt to examine them more closely. He peered through the lens of his magnifying glass, noting the scratches would have been made by footwear with steel tips and heels. The lines were initially straight, suggesting the wearer had been applying force in the direction of the shallow gouges. Then the scratches twisted, as the foot had turned for more grip. He measured the distance between the scratches and noted these in his book. He stood back, imagining the actions of the bodies involved in the life-or-death competition.

The glass from the broken window still lay on the floor - a radiated pattern scattered two to three feet from where the breakage had occurred. He made more notes, then left.

Upstairs, Locke-Croft checked the spare bedroom and agreed with the police report that the room appeared not to have been utilised for some time. He noticed fresh scratches in the floorboards. Viewing them closely, he noted they had been made by soles similar to those discovered in the sitting room. They were shallower than the ones he'd just examined downstairs. He measured the distance between the marks created by the metal toe and heel tips, then recorded these.

In the bathroom two Addis, bone-handled, bristle tooth-brushes stood in a blue flower-patterned white china tumbler. A single man would not need two of these pricy brushes. He must share his residence with another from time to time. Someone who, going by the unused spare bedroom, also shared his bed.

The main bedroom was larger than the spare, its three-quarter bed topped by a walnut headboard, matched by a shorter footboard in the same veneer. On the dressing table, two objects gave away the feminine company: the perfume bottle, which he recognised at once by its aroma, and a long-handled hairbrush. The china brush had a similar pattern to the tumbler in the bathroom but had yellow and rose-coloured corolla. Most definitely a lady's brush. The magnifying glass came out again, and he examined the hairs trapped within its bristles. He extracted three long silky hairs, their shade that of a horse chestnut seed.

He recalled his first autumnal conker fight with his older brother, Michael, when he was just five years old. They had drilled holes through the centres and fed string into them, tying a large knot to hold the conker in place. He tried to hit his brother's but only managed a weak, glancing blow. Then he'd held his conker string still as his brother whacked it with all his strength, splitting it into pieces. He remembered crying. Not just because his brother had yet again demonstrated his superiority, but because he'd hated to see the conker smashed, its glossy, grained mahogany beauty destroyed.

He placed the hairs inside a small pouch, then continued his scrutiny of the room.

"Sir," came the shout from downstairs. Smith came running upstairs looking for him. He was holding a five-inch bladed knife, matching those in the kitchen block. He was grinning with his success. "I found it in the drain just up the street. I had to reach in deep, while the PC held my legs." His wet and grimy arms confirmed his story. So did the smell of stagnant water.

"Well done, Smith. Well done, indeed. Excellent work. Bag it up, then take it into Scotland Yard and have the laboratory check it for fingerprints and anything else that might link it to the crime."

"Will do, sir. Are we finished for the day? Only it's getting late and my wife will expect me home for dinner."

"Hmm... The laboratory will be closed, so there's no point you going to the Yard with it this evening. But it's too important for you to take it home. Lodge the evidence with *your* station before going for dinner, then collect it tomorrow and get it to the forensics team by 9am in the morning. After you've done that, report to my accommodation. I shall expect you by 10:30am."

Smith looked deep in thought, probably assessing his ability to meet those timings, before responding. "Yes, sir. Will you be leaving now? The PC needs to know."

"Indeed I will, Smith. Please inform the constable that he can lock up and take the key back to the station after I leave. Now that I've finished examining the crime scene, it no longer needs to be guarded."

They both exited the mews house and Locke-Croft wandered up the street, noting the two policemen had left in the other direction. He knocked on a door and when it opened, he flashed a badge to the occupant as he notified him he was with the Metropolitan Police. The man was unhelpful, and his enquiries continued to be unsuccessful until he reached Number 11.

A diminutive lady with grey hair opened the door. She had wire-rimmed glasses perched on her nose, but she looked over them at the visitor. The skirt of her dress reached down to her ankles and its bodice finished in a high neckline.

"Good day to you, ma'am. Detective Locke-Croft, with the Met. You may have heard that last week Mr Finchley at Number 7 met with an untimely end?"

"Oh dear. Yes, I did hear. It's rather worrying. This is such a quiet street. I've never known a crime to be committed here. How can I help you?"

"Were you at home around 1pm on this day last week?"

"Oh, most definitely. I rarely go out nowadays. My friends call in for a game of bridge once a week and my nephew calls in to see me, monthly."

"Do you not even venture out to buy your food?"

"Oh no! The butcher and baker deliver weekly, and a man from the fruit and veg market brings my food on Wednesdays and Saturdays."

"Did you notice anything unusual the day that Finchley was murdered?"

"My chair is near the window, so I normally see anyone passing by. The postman was on his rounds about 9:30, and-"

"What about later in the day? Say, after 12 o'clock?"

"Let me think... A police constable walked past about 12:30. The next time I spotted someone was at... 1pm. A young man ran past my window."

"How do you know it was 1pm?"

"I had been listening to a drama on the wireless. It had just finished, and the 1 o'clock pips were sounding when the man passed by."

"Did you see him? Are you able to describe his clothing or anything about his feature or build?" She didn't immediately respond, so he added: "perhaps you were unable to make out any detail," Locke-Croft suggested, eyeing her glasses.

"My eyesight's not so good nowadays, I admit. I need to wear spectacles to read or do my embroidery, but they're still fine for seeing more distant things. He had a long nose. I saw it clearly in profile. He looked skinny – his cheek bones were prominent. But I cannot tell you anything else about him. It was just a flash as he ran past my window."

"I am utterly amazed at the detail you've provided already, ma'am. I am most obliged. In which direction was the man running?"

"He came from my left and ran down the street, towards Number 7, where the murder occurred."

Locke-Croft noted this in his pocketbook. This concurred with Goldsworthy's report, from his talk with the lady at Number 2. He wondered why the DC had not also spoken with *this* lady, given that she rarely left home. "Can you tell me anything about Mr Finchley?"

"I seldom see him. I think he works somewhere to the south from here, so doesn't normally pass my door. He looks like a respectable young man, but I've never spoken to him."

"For the records, ma'am: your name, please?"

"Mrs Fenchurch, Gloria. I'm a widow, now. My husband left me almost ten years ago; heart attack. I told him-"

"Thank you so much for your time, Mrs Fenchurch. Most helpful." He turned and walked away before she could divulge any more of her history.

By the time Locke-Croft reached Number 8, he'd discovered nothing of significance about Finchley. He hoped someone would be at home, as the house was directly across the road from Finchley's abode.

A middle-aged man with dark curly hair opened the door. He had a broad face with deep-set eyes. "Yes?"

"Sorry to trouble you, sir. I'm with the Met." He flashed the badge. "You will undoubtedly have heard that one week ago James Finchley was murdered in the house just across the road?"

"Yes. Ghastly!"

"Were you at home that day, sir?"

"Not during the day. I leave home at 8:30am on weekdays and do not return until the evening."

"Did you know Mr Finchley?"

"Only in passing. We're not friends."

"So, you've not been inside his house, then?"

"Only once."

"And was that recently?"

"About two weeks ago, actually. He invited me in for a glass of port."

"What do you know of the man? Employment? Hobbies and pastimes? Associations? Relationships?"

"As I said, I hardly know him. But I can tell you he has lady friends call on him in the evenings. I've occasionally seen women leaving his house at breakfast time."

"Has he had any men call?"

"Not that I've noticed?"

"These women who call at his house... are they young or old?

How are they dressed? Are they beautiful or plain?"

"I've seen three different women - one stunningly beautiful, in her mid-twenties I'd say, smartly dressed but not expensively so." He thought for a minute. "The next oldest of the three would be in her early thirties, attractive but not beautiful. She dressed more elegantly, and in better quality clothing than the younger woman. I noted the third woman had long, lustrous auburn hair. It shimmered in the light. I expect she was nearer forty years of age."

"Anything else you can recall?"

"I noticed the auburn-haired lady leaving one morning, so got a better look at her. She was gorgeous. Not a classic beauty, like the younger one, but exotic, sexy. She had dark eyes and light brown skin."

"Do you remember when this over-night stay occurred?"

"Recently. Perhaps a week ago. Wait... Yes, of course. It was on the day of Finchley's murder."

"Thank you, sir. Most enlightening. Your name, please?"

"Anderson. John Anderson."

"Most obliged, Mr Anderson." He turned and walked away, satisfied to have learned something of interest.

* * *

Locke-Croft headed back toward Regent's Park, via Brunswick Place. He didn't trust the police reports, so stopped at some houses and enquired whether anyone had seen the fugitive being chased. He noted the hunted man's description, given by the few people who'd seen him.

On completion of his enquiries, he entered Regent's Park and headed west, letting his mind wander as he strolled towards his home. He exited the park at its southwest corner, crossed the road, and was soon back in his apartment. Despite the lightness of the spring evening, his home was shaded. Tall townhouses in the row behind obscured the early evening sunshine that would otherwise have illuminated his sitting room. This gloom didn't bother him, however. His mind had more important things to keep it occupied.

He pondered what he'd found so far. Other than the supposed theft of candelabra, there was no apparent motive, and the detectives had not suggested one in their reports. The fugitive chased from the scene appeared to be innocent. He'd need to know more about James Finchley. Tomorrow he would speak with work colleagues, and perhaps family. A motive for the homicide would help track down the murderer.

He picked up his violin and began to play. Anyone passing on the street below would think a professional violinist was practising for his next concert performance. He lost himself in the music, the facts of the crime whirling around in his sub-conscious mind.

* * *

25th May

Over breakfast Locke-Croft read the Times newspaper to keep up with current affairs. The most notable news was that Britain had severed diplomatic ties with the Soviet Union. There were accusations of espionage and sedition. He'd noticed that since Stalin's rise to power, interference in other country's affairs appeared to have multiplied.

He contemplated the socialist system. Locke-Croft understood the case for communism – equality of status and reward, and the joint ownership of property. It annoyed him immensely that much of the United Kingdom was in the hands of extraordinarily wealthy landowners. People who'd inherited land and properties. Many of these earlier generations had been gifted the land for services to the Crown, or perhaps taken it by force, coercion or fraud.

But socialism and the single party system in reality meant dictatorship. It resulted in a lack of choice over who governed the country and what rules society wished to live by. Instead, those in unelected power made the decisions. Although the democratic system was flawed, at least the people got *some* say in how the country was run.

Locke-Croft placed the paper on his side table and considered yesterday's inquiries. He wondered why Harrison was a detective of repute, given his inadequate investigation of the crime scene, and the little follow up work.

After breakfast, he examined the evidence and re-read the police reports. Richards' account provided little detail about the man chased from the scene. Moreover, his questioning of residents of Brunswick Place had proven unsuccessful. And the constable lacked the determination to catch the fugitive. Why?

Goldsworthy had noted interesting points about the expensive furniture in a modest house and the missing knife from the kitchen. But he'd not searched for this missing blade – such a blatant hole in the investigation. The detective constable's questioning of mews' residents *had* been useful, but the officer had not looked into the character of the victim. No one had sought alternative motives for the crime.

Inspector Harrison's report was lengthy. It stated on arrival at the scene he'd found uniformed constables gathering near a house with a broken window. He took control of the situation, entered the house by the unlocked door and found the body, which had suffered a fatal wound to the throat. Harrison had noted multiple points about the crime scene but then jumped to a simple conclusion of a theft, gone wrong. He would speak with these policemen and endeavour to drag further information from their minds.

At 10:30am, Constable Smith arrived. "Good morning, Smith. Take a seat. I'll be with you in a minute."

Smith sat but didn't relax. There was always a tension when in Locke-Croft's presence, and he had a confession to make, when Locke-Croft allowed him to speak. He waited for the man's next directive, which came quickly.

"I have interviews to conduct today: three policemen and a pathologist for a start. Come, Smith. We shall take the Bakerloo

Line. Oh, and you'll need this," he said, passing him his police badge that he'd stolen from him the previous day. "You must have dropped it in the mews."

"Thank you, sir." Smith's frown left him. "I was extremely worried when I found it missing this morning. In fact, I spent ages searching my house for it before leaving. I wasn't able to go to the crime laboratory with the knife, as they'd have not let me into the building. I still have it here," he said, extracting it from his pocket.

"Not to worry, Smith. We're heading there now, anyway."

They arrived at Scotland Yard half an hour later and marched into the Met headquarters. He knocked and walked into the office of DCI Weatherspoon. "Chief Inspector. I need to speak with your men regarding their reports on the Finchley murder. Please arrange for them to meet with me without delay."

"Good day to you, Mr Locke-Croft. More notice would have been helpful. If you'd telephoned earlier, I'd have made arrangements. I cannot be certain any of the three officers will be available. Please take a seat and I will enquire as to their whereabouts."

The DCI left the office in search of Harrison and Goldsworthy. Locke-Croft waited until the chief inspector had disappeared down the corridor before rising. He wandered around the room, perusing the information on its walls, then shuffled through the documents on the inspector's desk.

"Sir, you shouldn't be looking at the DCI's documents," Smith piped up.

"Quiet, Smith. You know my rules. There may be information here relevant to this crime or the people investigating it." He continued his search, stopping when he saw that PC Richards had been recommended for transfer to the detective branch.

Another document proposed DC Goldsworthy should be put forward for his sergeant's exam. He returned to his chair and sat just before Weatherspoon re-entered his office, with Harrison in tow.

"Goldsworthy is carrying out enquiries related to another case, so is unavailable. Richards is on the beat, but Inspector Harrison can help you with your enquiries. I must attend a meeting, so you're welcome to use my office for the next hour if you wish."

"Thank you, Chief Inspector. Most helpful."

Weatherspoon grabbed some documents from his desk and left the room. Locke-Croft at once took the DCI's chair and invited Harrison to sit opposite him.

"Inspector. I read your report on the Finchley case, along with those written by your subordinates. What I require from you now is a verbal briefing on the case, during which I may ask clarification questions. Please proceed."

Harrison looked unhappy but did as instructed, referring to his notebook.

After allowing Harrison to speak for some time, Locke-Croft interrupted: "I can understand your assumption that a thief had taken the candelabra, given the dust rings on the sideboard. But wonder why no one noticed the suspect carrying any such items. The rings were large, suggesting the candelabra were bulky. They would have been difficult to hide. Your thoughts, Harrison?"

"I'd not thought of that, sir."

"Your report suggests your prime suspect is the man seen running from the mews. Pray tell me what you or your team have done to find this person?"

"We had a loose description of the fugitive and knew the direction he ran in, so we carried out house to house enquiries along the route taken. But other than the one person in Brunswick Place who'd seen him and offered a description, we got nowhere."

"Yes. Goldsworthy's witness said she'd seen the man before, at the market in Camden. What resulted from your enquiries in Camden, inspector?"

"Goldsworthy visited the borough and spoke to some traders, but no one admitted to knowing the suspect. He drew a blank."

"And what action did you take following this failure, inspector?"

"There wasn't much more to be done. We had no other leads and Camden was a dead end."

"If the chief constable had not invited me to progress this case, what line of action would you have taken next?"

"As you will know from my report, we checked with pawn shops in the area for any candelabra that had recently been offered for sale. But again, this led nowhere. We also tracked down the hansom cab driver, whose horse nearly knocked down the suspect. He concurred with the man's description, but nothing else."

"Please answer my question, inspector. What would have been your *next* move?"

"Another examination of the crime scene was on my to do list. And I planned to speak personally with neighbours in the mews, hoping that they might shed some light on Finchley's character and habits."

"Very good, Harrison, but why have you not already done so? Were you sleeping on duty? What else should you have already done?"

Harrison stuttered as he tried to respond to Locke-Crofts accusations and queries. He chose to ignore the accusations.

63

"F-f-following from the neighbour enquiries, I planned to speak with his colleagues and employers. As the theft motive has led us nowhere, I had intended to consider other motives."

"Again, Harrison, why had you not already carried out these enquiries? I cannot comprehend how you spent your time when you were on the case."

Harrison remained silent.

"There's no further merit to continuing discussions with you, inspector. I shall continue my investigations and return later today to speak with Goldsworthy. You must ensure he is available for when I return at 2pm. Come, Smith."

He rose from the DCI's chair and left the room, leaving Harrison floundering.

* * *

Locke-Croft flagged down an Austin cab, then boarded along with Smith. "Weymouth Street. The offices of Chippenham and Dudley Solicitors."

"Right-o, guv."

Locke-Croft sat in silence throughout the journey, apparently looking out of the window but actually staring into space, as his mind rehearsed his questions. On arrival, he paid the driver and stepped out of the cab. The offices were within a four storey, red bricked Victorian townhouse. Its grand entrance door, with arched transom light, was shaded by a sandstone gabled portico.

He entered through the unlocked door and found the reception in a room to the left. "Good afternoon. Detective Locke-Croft. I'm with the Metropolitan Police."

Smith kept quiet but was ready to show his badge if necessary.

"What can I do for you, detective?" the middle-aged man

behind the counter asked.

Locke-Croft quickly assessed his attire, features, and demeanour. Although his clothing was formal, clean, and well pressed, going by the worn fabric, his suit must have been many years old – suggesting he was not paid well for his duties. The man was subservient and willing to please, drawing pleasure from being efficient and effective in his work. He glanced at the man's desk, noting a triangular name plaque.

"Mr Sharpe. I expect you are aware of Mr James Finchley's demise. You shall of course wish to help me find the gentleman's killer. So I would be grateful if you would answer my questions."

"Certainly, sir. What a dreadful business. A constable called in last week to break the news. We cannot understand why anyone would wish to kill Mr Finchley. He was a very personable chap."

"Other than his likeability, what more can you tell me about Finchley? His character? Any associates? How he dressed?"

"Well, sir. I don't know what he did in his spare time; perhaps one of the partners might have more knowledge than me. I can tell you, however, he always dressed smartly. He was prompt, diligent and courteous. Mr Finchley never kept his clients waiting, and they invariably left with a smile on their faces – unless they'd come about a dire matter, of course. The women, in particular, seemed to like his manner."

"I must view his client list and his diary for the last year. His killer may have been someone he knew through work or otherwise."

"Please take a seat, and I'll find the information you need, sir."

"I must speak with the partners, individually, Mr Sharpe, so before you start on this work, please make arrangements."

"The partners all have clients with them. But..." Just then a man came down the stairs and left the building. "Ah! Mr Dudley should be free, now. His next appointment is not for another ten minutes."

He left his counter and went to speak with the partner, returning swiftly. "He will meet with you now. Please go up. First door on the right. It should be open. I'll get together the information you requested while you're speaking with him and look for an opportunity for you to meet with Mr Chippenham."

"That's most helpful, Mr Sharpe. Your employers must value you highly for your efficiency and cooperation."

Sharpe smiled, enjoying the praise, and at once started work on satisfying the detective's request.

"Mr Dudley, I presume," he said, on entering the first-floor office.

"Indeed, sir. And you are?"

"Locke-Croft. With the Met. This is Detective Constable Smith." Smith showed his badge, thinking it the right thing to do.

"Gentlemen, please sit... What can I do for you? I understand you're investigating James Finchley's murder." The leather chair creaked as Locke-Croft sat but felt solid and stable, nonetheless. He could detect the smell of fresh beeswax polish that must have been recently applied to the leather desk writing surface, going by its sheen.

"That's correct. It is necessary to understand the man's character and learn of his associations, if we are to ascertain the motive for this murder and identify suspects."

"Do you not yet have someone in custody?"

"No, Mr Dudley, but fear not, we will have the murderer soon. Please enlighten me about Mr Finchley. His background. His personality. Any known associations, hobbies and pastimes.

The more you can tell me, the better."

Dudley did as he was requested but divulged little of interest. It would appear that Finchley was of exemplary character. But what he did outside the office was unknown.

* * *

Locke-Croft returned to the reception, and Mr Sharpe promptly stood on seeing the detective. "I have all you asked for here, sir," he said, passing Locke-Croft an envelope containing documents.

"Thank you, Sharpe. Most helpful. One last question. Do any of these names ring any bells with you?" he asked, handing Sharpe a list.

"Richards is the only name I recognise, sir. He and his wife are on Mr Chippenham's client list."

"Have the Richards been here within the last six months?"

"Most definitely, sir. I couldn't forget this couple, as Mrs Richards is most beautiful. It was recent, but I'll need to check."

Locke-Croft stood observing all around him as Sharpe carried out his research. On Sharpe's desk a row of erasers sat, lined up as if a game of dominos were in play. His pencils all showed signs of recent sharpening and his ink pen sat neatly central on a small blotting pad. The man evidently favoured precision and order. Locke-Croft concluded he could rely on the accuracy of whatever Sharpe told him.

"I've noted down the dates of their appointments," he said, passing Locke-Croft a slip of paper.

"Is it possible that Mr and Mrs Richards came into contact with James Finchley?"

"Why, yes. Although their appointment was with Mr Chippenham, he was waylaid on the day of their first appointment, so I showed them into Mr Finchley's office, as he was free. On the next visit I made the appointment with Mr Finchley – for continuity."

"I see. Can you tell me anything else about these visits?"

"Only that, on the second visit, Mrs Richards came alone. She said her husband had been called into work."

"Hmm... thank you."

"Mr Chippenham can see you now, sir."

"Excellent."

The result of Locke-Croft's interview with Chippenham was much the same as his discussion with Mr Dudley. Before returning to Scotland Yard, he had one final question for the solicitor's clerk. "Mr Sharpe."

"Sir?"

"The day that Finchley was murdered was a Wednesday. And the murder occurred around 1pm. Surely he would have been at work at that time?"

"Ah! Yes. That day he phoned in about 9am to say he was under the weather and would be unable to come into the office but would do some work from home."

"Thank you, Mr Sharpe." Locke-Croft turned and marched out of the offices, with Smith at his heels.

* * *

"Ah! Goldsworthy," Locke-Croft declared as he entered the DCI's office just after 2pm. "I need you to recall all you know about the Finchley case."

"Haven't you read my report, sir?"

"Yes, yes. But reports invariably leave out detail that might be important."

"Very well. I received a call from Inspector Harrison shortly after 1pm, requesting my assistance at Park Square Mews. It took me about twenty minutes to reach the address. So I'll have arrived about half one. PC Richards was there assisting the inspector, but Harrison dismissed him soon after my arrival."

"Go on."

Goldsworthy reported his findings in the kitchen and dining room, much as he had written in his formal report, concluding with mentioning the dust-free rings to his boss.

"And what was the inspector's reaction when you mentioned the possible missing candelabra?"

"He at once concluded that the murderer had been a thief who'd broken into the house but was disturbed after pocketing the candelabra. He concluded that a fight resulted in Finchley being murdered and the thief-cum-murderer escaped the way he had come, through the broken window."

"Do you agree with the inspector's supposition?"

"It was possible... I suppose."

"Why do you doubt?"

"The thief would have had to break the sitting room window-pane, climb through the opening, go into the kitchen and take the knife, before moving into the dining room. Why would he do that? Then he would have removed the two candelabra and be leaving the room when Finchley turned up. The fight perhaps progressed into the sitting room, but if the intruder had the knife, surely he would have slashed and stabbed at Finchley from the front?"

"Indeed, Goldsworthy. A sliced throat suggests a surprise attack from behind, not a fight." He paused before asking the next question. "Did the inspector engage you in discussion on any other motives or scenarios?"

"No, sir."

"What further enquiries did you make?"

"I spoke with neighbours and found a lady at Number 2 who'd seen the man running out of the mews. Her description matched with Richard's report."

"And."

"Richards helped me with door-to-door enquiries along Brunswick Place. We found one witness, who concurred with the description. She even suggested she'd seen him before. I followed up on that lead by visiting the market at Camden, but no one admitted to knowing him. So that was a dead end."

"Hmm."

"That's all there is, sir. Oh, not quite. I also visited the firm that Finchley work for but they weren't able to tell me anything about his life outside work."

"If you had been in charge of the investigation, what would you have done next?"

Goldsworthy explained the lines of investigation he would undertake, if he were in charge of the investigation.

Conscious that he still needed to speak with the uniformed PC before the day was out, Locke-Croft wound up his conversation. He complemented Goldsworthy on his deductions, even though he hadn't shown outstanding detective talent, and suggested he'd make a good sergeant. Then he sent him away with a smile on his face.

* * *

"Richards, I'm told you were the officer who raised the alarm about the murder at Park Square Mews. Tell me about that day and leave out no detail."

70

Richards knew the detective was not a police officer but had the chief constable's authority to investigate the crime. He referred to his notebook to clarify facts, then reported all that had happened. It mostly matched with the report that he'd filed.

"I hear you wish to become a detective?"

"Yes, sir. I enjoy patrolling the streets, but I believe I'd impact crime more if I became a detective."

"Given your poor physical fitness, you are perhaps better suited to investigations than chasing criminals."

"What do you mean, sir? I walk the streets eight hours a day and I've caught many a petty criminal."

"But you failed to keep up with the suspect who ran from Park Square Mews and you gave up the chase just a short distance from the scene – at Regent's Park. Out of breath, I'm told."

"I wasn't out of breath, sir. My boots had slipped on the cobbles and I'd fallen, winding myself."

"But why does your report say you lost the fugitive in the woods?"

"I didn't want to admit my failure to keep up with the man, so I suggested that he'd given me the slip."

"So you say! Another anomaly I need to close, Richards. You said you found a three-ringed lapel badge on the floor of the crime scene and gave it to Inspector Harrison, yet this was not in your report. Why?"

"I didn't think to mention it, as I was merely assisting the inspector. My expectation was that *he* would log the badge in *his* report. I'm not a detective yet, so only reported on my involvement as a beat copper."

"Hmm... You also mentioned speaking with the inspector about the window catch. You thought perhaps it was jammed. I suppose you left that out of your report for the same reason you didn't mention the lapel badge – correct?"

"Yes, sir."

"If you do become a detective, Richards, you will need to be more diligent in writing your reports – leaving out nothing. It is often the minor details that provide clues to solving a crime. Does anything else comes to mind – something you've not yet reported?"

Richards thought for a while before responding. "There's nothing else, sir."

"Right, be off with you then."

* * *

26th May

At ten the next morning, Locke-Croft met his official escort at the mortuary. The Victoriana building was red brick, with sash windows. Its youth was obvious as the paintwork was still fresh, with no sign of multiple coats seen on older buildings. "Good day to you, Smith."

"Good morning, sir. Another fine day, don't you think?"

"It *is* helpful to not be drenched or frozen but being dry and sunny doesn't actually help solve the case. Let us proceed."

Smith pondered why Locke-Croft was such a serious-minded fellow. What might have happened in his past to create this attitude, he wondered? He'd not seen the man draw any pleasure from his duties and never seen even a hint of a smile.

They entered the building and were shown through to the mortuary. The room reminded Locke-Croft of a spacious public toilet. The usual human waste smells mingled with disinfectant and bleach. Typically, the room was devoid of all but the necessary furniture. The walls were white tiled, and the floor covered in a green linoleum. As the door closed behind him, Locke-Croft noticed a lapel badge with three oval interlinking rings attached to the coat hanging there.

"Good day to you, Dr Williams... Has your examination of Finchley's body been completed?"

"Yes. I've just signed the report. Would you like to read it?"

"Indeed, I would."

The doctor passed him a copy and Locke-Croft sat on a chair in the pathologist's office, taking in the details. Ten minutes later, he emerged from the office and approached the doctor. "May I examine the body?"

"You may. The investigating officer has that right, but I can't imagine what that would achieve." He led the detective to the corpse, despite his scepticism. "Are you trained in autopsy, Mr Locke-Croft?"

"No, but I have studied the science and I'm aware of the signs a cadaver can display, and what these reveal."

Doctor Williams squeezed his lips together and furrowed his brow as he considered Locke-Croft's response.

He examined Finchley's body. The throat incision was deep at one side of the neck but tapered out at the other. He called to the pathologist. "Doctor Williams. You didn't say in your report, but would you agree that the wound in Finchley's throat was made from right to left?"

"Yes. I would. Thank you for spotting my omission, Mr Locke-Croft. I shall make that addition to the report."

"I note that there were no cuts to the deceased's hands. Your report doesn't explain this. Pray tell what you deduced from his undamaged hands?"

"Where has my mind been today? I can't believe I missed reporting on that matter. It would suggest the victim had not defended himself against the knife attack. The assailant must have surprised him."

"And what of the cutting angle, doctor?"

"What do you mean?"

"It is clear to me the incision was not horizontal but sliced upwards as it cut into Finchley's throat. Best you add that into the report, as well, doctor."

"I will. I will." Williams looked flustered.

"Doctor. I note in your report that you believe the cut was made by a large knife. Is that correct?"

"Yes. That's my opinion. Why?"

Locke-Croft ignored the question, handed the report back to the doctor, bid him good day, and left.

"Smith. I have some tasks for you to complete between now and when we meet tomorrow morning. You must be discreet in how these are conducted, otherwise, you might raise suspicions."

"Right, sir. What is it you want me to do?"

After briefing the detective, Locke-Croft instructed him to be at the main entrance to Scotland Yard at 10:30 the next morning.

* * *

The Test - Afterword

Dear Reader, by now you should have deduced who might have murdered the victim, how and why. Now read the attached appendices, reach your conclusion, and provide a written answer. If you correctly solve this conundrum, you will have done well, and I salute you.

* * *

Hicks placed *The Test* back into its envelope, satisfied that it was all readable and clear. The scenario painted by its author hadn't made it obvious who killed Finchley. It didn't seem likely that the suspect identified by the police had committed the crime. Three of the four law officers, though, could perhaps be considered under suspicion. But Hicks had no inkling of who had committed murder nor why, and he did not understand how to reduce the choice, let alone identify the guilty person.

By now it was late, so he left reading of the *Solution* and the appendices to another time. He rose from his chair and went in search of his wife.

* * *

In the morning Hicks walked the short distance from his home to the nearby company offices, carrying his attaché case containing the client's documents. He was keen to get the mundane processes completed this morning, to free him for further reading. By lunchtime he was pleasantly surprised that the sun had burnt off the mist and was brightening the green in Portman Square. Rather than sit longer in his office, Hicks took his case and left the building, informing his secretary where to find him, if needed.

He sat on a bench in the park, removed from his case the lunch his wife had provided, then laid a large cotton napkin over his lap, ready to eat. He extracted the appendices and scanned these prior to removing the *Solution* from its envelope. While taking the first bite of his roast beef and horseradish sandwich, Hicks began to read.

* * *

III

Part Three

The Solution

The Solution - Foreword

I have written the Solution as a concluding part to the short story 'Murder in the Mews' which detailed the crime and subsequent investigation. Evidence presented in this narrative is supported by documents as appendices. These include: the post-mortem and police reports, records obtained from other sources, notes of my meetings with various persons, and details of physical evidence.

I expect explanations offered by those taking the test to expose the culprit, their opportunity, motive, means and evidence, in whatever form they wish. Provided they match reasonably closely with the solution detailed here, that will be satisfactory.

* * *

27th May

"So, Silvester, have you made progress in identifying the killer?" the chief constable asked, as Locke-Croft entered his office, shaking the water from his coat.

"I have, Charles. In fact, I need you to gather all your officers involved with the investigation, so I may interrogate them."

"What do you mean: *interrogate* them?"

"I believe they have not been forthcoming with all the facts of the case, and I must extract information from them to identify the culprit."

"Oh! I see. I thought you were suggesting one of my officers was the murderer."

Locke-Croft handed a list to the chief constable. "These are the people who I require gathered together. Shall we say 11am?"

He took the list and scanned down it before agreeing to order their attendance. Locke-Croft spun on his heels and marched out of the station. He met with DC Smith outside and discussed the results of his investigations and Smith's duties later that day.

* * *

"Gentlemen," Locke-Croft grabbed the attention of those gathered. "I asked for you all to be brought together today, as I know who committed the murder and I intend to reveal him to you before the hour is out."

All ears and eyes focused on Locke-Croft.

Locke-Croft surveyed the faces, noting the expressions and demeanour, knowing that body language gave away so much about the individual.

Inspector Harrison was looking sheepish, and rightly so. As the senior investigating officer, he had failed to make decent progress in the case, and he'd made no arrests.

Goldsworthy appeared impatient. Perhaps he was keen to get back to investigating the crime?

Constable Richards looked to be pleased to be having a rest in the warm, instead of pounding his beat in the driving rain. There was a mustiness to the room, and the windows had steamed up.

Dr Williams fidgeted with his bag, his left hand opening and closing the catch. He looked furtively around the room, avoiding eye contact with the consulting detective.

DCI Weatherspoon sat with his legs crossed and his hands resting on his knees. He glanced at his pocket watch, suggesting he had other things he needed to do or places to be.

Superintendent Bateman's cheeks were pulled in, his face taught. It appeared he didn't enjoy having an amateur taking over from his own detectives.

The chief constable stared at Locke-Croft in anticipation. He had newspaper reporters pushing for updates, and Lord Finchley on his back. But he had nothing to offer.

"Gentlemen, let me replay the crime to you and the following investigation." He paused, looking around at the faces present, then continued. "At about 1pm on the 20th May 1927, one James Finchley was murdered by a deep cut to the throat, administered from behind using a sharp instrument. None of the neighbours heard a struggle, but from the room's disarray, it seemed one *had* taken place."

After a short pause, he continued. "According to the investigation report, the victim disturbed the intruder whilst he was taking two silver candelabra from the dining room. But they had fought in the sitting room. The thief turned murderer, was reported to have broken the window in that room and climbed through it to make his escape."

He scanned the room again, gauging the thoughts of each person. The Superintendent looked as if he were thinking 'get on with it.' Others were looking curious, their interest piqued.

"But gentlemen, why would the murderer break the window and climb out through the jagged glass stuck in the frame, when he could have just walked through the unlocked door? I examined the glass from the broken window and noted that there were no fragments of cloth present and no sign of any blood. I found this unlikely, given the small opening and the man's haste to leave the scene."

"Two circular dust-free marks on the dining room sideboard had given rise to the theft, gone wrong theory. But Finchley's parents could not remember such items adorning their son's sideboard when they last visited."

He let the audience absorb what he'd said before going on. "Furthermore, the dust-free rings had been made by human hand." Again, he paused. The chief constable's mouth was open as he absorbed this statement.

"PC Richards was on foot patrol around this time and heard the window breaking. He said he'd seen a person emerge from the mews and run off, so shouted for the man to stop and sounded his whistle. He gave chase, assuming the running man was a criminal – his hasty escape and refusal to stop confirming this assumption."

"Richard's report states the suspect ran up Brunswick Place, along Ulster Terrace, then into Regent's Park, where he gave him the slip in a wooded area. The constable returned to the scene and reported to the officer in charge, Inspector Harrison, who enlisted his help to investigate the crime scene."

He paused yet again as he gathered his thoughts. "The reports later made by these two officers of the law did not record *everything* that occurred during their investigations. But when I later spoke with them, further detail arose that shaped my thinking."

"Richards had not noticed footprints beneath the broken window, and Harrison's report made no mention of these either. But when I examined the area, which had been cordoned off since the event, I noticed only one set of prints: size 11 boots. On inspecting these prints it became clear that the wearer of the boots had approached the window from outside, then walked away. Later, the same feet had returned and left again. Strange patterning for a man escaping the scene in a hurry!"

"The fugitive chased by PC Richards was of medium height and slim build. He ran with great speed and agility. Two neighbours, at No. 2 and No. 11, had also seen a person of this description, running down the street past the crime scene. On checking when these events had occurred, I found them to be coincidental. It was evident that the man had *not* left No 7 and run out of the mews just as Richards arrived. He had come from further up the street and could not be our murderer. Furthermore, a male of slim build and medium height will possess medium size feet – perhaps 8 or 9. Not 11."

The gathered faces all looked aghast, except one, confirming

Locke-Croft's suspicions. "So, we are looking for another person. A man with size 11 feet." Locke-Croft noticed the officer unconsciously move his feet backwards under his chair.

"The motive for the attack is uncertain. The candelabra may have never existed and nothing else appeared to be missing. There was even a £20 note in the victim's wallet. We must then look for another motive. As we all know, the main motives for cold blooded murder are jealousy, revenge for disloyalty or removal of a competitor, monetary gain and hatred. Aside from these normal motives, are those committed by evil people – so called psychopaths. Could we perhaps be looking for someone who kills for pleasure?"

He let the suggestion hang before continuing. "We should also not yet discount the crime of passion. One not planned but brought about by circumstances. Or perhaps a fight that escalated. Unplanned, but just as deadly."

Another pause. "But I believe the perpetrator of this crime visited the premises intent on doing harm to the victim. Had the man killed his opponent in an unplanned, provoked brawl, he would most likely have run out the front door, not staged a pretend escape through the broken window. There would likely have also been more disarray and broken furniture in the sitting room. Thus, I believe there was planning involved in this murder."

The facial expressions before him gave away the perplexed minds of the law officers.

"Was Finchley's murder the work of a serial killer? No! A psychopath enjoys the game of proving his superiority and loves to leave clues. You will no doubt be aware of killers who left articles in the pockets of their victims, items stuffed up noses or lodged in their throats, or sometimes just laid on the cadaver. Often these psychopaths will stage the body to look like other crimes. But Finchley's body wasn't staged, and no clues had been left. No. This murderer killed for personal gain, not pleasure."

"Let us re-examine the facts – some that may lead to the culprit but others which might be red herrings. Richards told me that when asked by Harrison why he thought the murderer had broken the glass to escape, instead of opening the window, he'd suggested the latch might have been stuck. The inspector tried the latch and found it was seized, confirming Richards' reasoning. But when I inspected the crime scene, I found the latch to be operational. Inspector Harrison, please explain this anomaly?"

Harrison sat up straight, frowning, then spoke forcefully. "What are you saying, sir? That I pretended the latch was jammed when all along it was free? Why would I falsify such a thing? When I tried the latch, it wouldn't move. Others may have tried it since and loosened it? What other explanation can there be?" He sat back into his chair again, with all eyes upon him.

"Another matter for you to answer, inspector: pray tell us why you are wearing a new coat?"

He shook his head in disbelief at the question before answering. "My old coat was worn out. I'd saved for months to afford a new one. What's that got to do with anything?"

"On the day of the murder, the coat you wore was too small. The sleeves didn't reach your wrists, the hem was above your knee, and it was tight around your chest. Had you grown several inches upwards and outwards while you were saving for the new coat, inspector?

"No. No, of course not. When I left home on the morning of

the crime, I was rushing and grabbed the wrong coat from the cloak cupboard. It was my brother-in-law's. He was staying with us at the time."

Locke-Croft pursed his lips, then turned from the officers to gather his thoughts. The explanation was plausible if his relative corroborated it. He turned again.

"Let us, for now, assume your explanation to be genuine."

Harrison looked peeved at not having his account accepted.

Locke-Croft resumed. "Hanging on a hook at No 7 Park Square Mews, was a coat, like the one recently bought by Inspector Harrison. And in my opinion a good size match with the inspector. On its left sleeve is dried blood. How did this blooded-sleeved coat – that could not be Finchley's – go unnoticed and unreported, Harrison?" he said, staring into his eyes.

"I never saw the coat you mention. I cannot comment further."

"So, you admit to being incompetent, inspector. Let me ask you another question. Do you recall being handed a lapel badge, retrieved from the floor of the sitting room by PC Richards?"

"No I do not. My mind was heavily occupied. If Richards handed my anything I do not recall."

Locke-Croft continued. "Richards did not note this evidence in his report but told me when questioned."

The PC nodded his head in confirmation.

"This lapel badge had three oval, intersecting rings. Does this mean something to any of you?" He waited one minute but there came no response. "This badge is the symbol of the Patriotic Order of Oddfellows. The triple links signify their motto of *Amicitia Amor et Veritas.* In English, gentlemen, this means friendship, love, and truth. The society promote themselves as a place for friendship and where members commit to helping each other in times of hardship. A good thing, I'm sure you'll agree."

He continued. "Of what import is this badge, then? It may have been the victim's, knocked off during the struggle, or perhaps been worn by the murderer. Either way, it is evidence, perhaps important, that has not been lodged and has now disappeared. It was last seen in your hand, inspector."

"This is ridiculous. What reason would I have had to hide this evidence – evidence that I do not even recall seeing, let alone possessing?"

"We shall see, inspector. Pray tell us what size boots you wear?"

Harrison jumped out of his seat. "What's going on here? Who is this incompetent civilian to come into Scotland Yard and start pointing fingers at the officer appointed to investigate the crime? My boots are size 11, as can be seen. That doesn't mean I had any involvement with the offence. I was at the scene. I examined the broken window from outside, so my boot prints would have been there. That proves *nothing*."

"Sit down, inspector. No need to get excited if you're inno-cent." Locke-Croft paused again. "Gentlemen, on becoming aware of the three-ringed lapel badge, I made some enquiries with Oddfellows' branches in the area. I found that James Finchley had belonged to the Warren Street branch. Dr Williams. To which branch do you belong?"

Williams looked flustered. "Err... I'm a member of North London Oddfellows in Camden."

"So you would *not* have known the deceased? The first time you'd have seen him would be when called to examine his body in Park Square Mews?"

"Yes. That's correct."

89

"Thank you, Doctor."

"Harrison. Please tell your colleagues where *you* hold Oddfellows membership?"

Instead of jumping to his feet again, he slumped back in his chair. "Mr Locke-Croft, why do you pursue me. I am an officer of the law. I was tasked with investigating this murder. How could I have committed it and for what reason?"

"Answer the question, Inspector," the chief constable commanded.

Harrison sat up, glared at the consulting detective, then did as directed. "I frequent the Warren Street branch." He slumped back into his seat, defeated.

"Gentlemen, these statements by Inspector Harrison raise questions in my mind. First, he chose to offer no answer when I asked about the three-ringed badge, yet he knew it to be a one worn by members of a society to which he belongs. Further, he was reluctant to respond when asked which branch of the society he belonged to. This evasion suggests he had something to hide."

He paused again, for effect. "The second question is that of him being tasked to investigate the crime. Chief Inspector, did you task Harrison with investigating this murder?"

Weatherspoon thought briefly before answering. "I did not formally appoint Harrison to the role, perhaps one of my superiors did?" He looked quizzically at the superintendent and chief constable, both of whom shook their heads to indicate they also had not formally tasked Harrison.

"Care to explain, Harrison, how you came to be the investigating officer?"

"Look. I might not have been *formally* tasked with the role, but I was the first detective on scene and assumed it. It was accepted that I would investigate because I'd already taken it upon myself."

"A bit of a coincidence, Inspector! You just happened to be in the area when the homicide was committed, and you hid evidence of your connection to the dead man. As you knew him, you should *not* have been the investigating officer. Your boot prints were the only ones found outside the supposed escape route. You tried to pass this crime off as a theft, gone wrong and took no action to pursue other motives. On the day of the incident, you wore a coat too short for you and had a new one the next day. And a coat that would fit you, but with blood on its sleeve, was discovered hanging in Finchley's cloakroom. But you conveniently did not notice this evidence. Too many coincidences, gentlemen."

Locke-Croft turned and paced around the room, his hands behind his back and his features set hard, with tight lips, wrinkled forehead and eyebrows furrowed.

* * *

The officers became impatient as two minutes passed, and the chief constable was about to say something when Locke-Croft swivelled and faced them again. "Let us now re-examine the motive for this crime. Might it have been greed? Monetary gain?"

He paused. "I had the dead man's account statements produced by his bank, and they are included in this evidence pack. James Finchley had around £1,000 in his accounts. Not an insubstantial sum. Perhaps worth killing for? But who stood to benefit from his death? He had no wife nor children to inherit his wealth. Nor had he a will and testament allocating his estate to anyone. So the law of probate would pass his remaining wealth to his parents. I very much doubt that Lord Finchley would need a meagre £1,000, given his *considerable* assets. It is safe to rule out inherited wealth as the motivation for murder. That leaves us with two of the most prevalent motives, gentlemen: jealousy and revenge."

"My examination of the house revealed that Mr Finchley had a female friend who stayed over with him. A lady who shared his bed. A woman who liked expensive perfume. Specifically, Shalimar. The name of this perfume comes from the *Gardens of Shalimar* in Lahore, Pakistan. Gardens created for Mumtaz Mahal, the woman for whom the Taj Mahal had also been built. It is not commonly available. In fact, it can only be purchased from a single store in London: Selfridges of Oxford Street. I enquired with the perfumery department and now possess a list of people who purchased this perfume within the last six months. One or two of the names on this list might surprise you?"

There was tension in the room, as they waited for the revelation.

"James Finchley was one of the customers and the other... was Dr Williams."

There was surprise on all the faces except the doctor's, who now looked worried.

"Curious, gentlemen, that the dead man, a member of Oddfellows, had recently bought this perfume. And Williams, who attended the crime and carried out the post-mortem on Finchley's body, was also an Oddfellow and a purchaser of the same quite rare perfume. Coincidences again, gentlemen... I do not believe in coincidences."

Harrison looked to be relieved that the focus had shifted to the doctor, but this was short lived when the detective turned back to him. "My nose is most sensitive, gentlemen, and can detect an aroma lingering on a person's clothing many days after contact with such perfume. Inspector Harrison, please tell us what perfume *your* spouse uses?

Harrison's jaw dropped open, shocked that he was again in the detective's spotlight. "I don't know what brand she uses. What could my wife have to do with this matter?"

"When I first met with you, Inspector, I smelled Shalimar on your clothes. I therefore deduced that your spouse must use the perfume. You frequent the same branch of the Oddfellows as the dead man, so it is inconceivable that you had not come in contact with him. Perhaps you introduced James Finchley to your wife at a function that included spouses. And he pursued her behind your back. Maybe we should send a constable to fetch Mrs Harrison now, to clarify this?"

"How dare you drag my wife into this. She can't afford such an expensive perfume. I doubt she's even set foot inside Selfridges, and she's never been to an Oddfellows function."

Locke-Croft paused and paced the room.

"As I said, I do not believe in coincidences. Let's suppose what I smelled on your person was lingering from when you had sniffed it in Finchley's bedroom. Let us accept for the moment that your wife has not used this perfume. That would not be true of Mrs Williams, would it, Doctor?"

"You are correct, detective. I did buy Shalimar for my wife, as a birthday present. She uses it most days. But what has that to do with this crime?"

"Let us suppose Mrs Williams were to meet young James Finchley at an Oddfellows gathering and fall for him..."

The doctor looked angry about the insinuation but kept quiet.

"Maybe Finchley invited her to his house on Park Square Mews and seduced her. This seduction perhaps led to an affair, an affair that became more than occasional pleasure between them. Finchley bought the perfume for Mrs Williams, so she could apply the same after their lovemaking to avoid suspicion on her return home.

This affair resulted in love. Love gained and love lost. Her love for her husband waned and her passion for Finchley grew until she could stand it no longer and confessed it, on the morning of the murder, after spending the night with her lover. She would leave the man she used to love, for the younger man..."

Williams leaped to his feet. "How dare you, sir? You denigrate the honour of my wife. Agatha is a lady of high morals. She would have nothing to do with this young fellow. I demand you retract this slander."

Locke-Croft looked unflinchingly into the doctor's eyes and said nothing. After a minute, the doctor sat down, his face red and puffed out.

"Tell me doctor, what is your wife's maiden name?"

Williams looked exasperated but answered. "Millarini."

"Ah! Italian. Does she possess chestnut eyes, light brown skin, and long lustrous auburn hair?"

Williams looked surprised to hear the accurate description of his spouse. "She does."

Locke-Croft turned to look at another officer. "Richards... You say you heard the window being broken, then at once a man ran out of the mews. Is that correct?"

"Yes, sir."

"Now. If I had been inside No 7 Park Square Mews and wanted to escape hurriedly from a crime scene, I would not break a window and climb out, when I could have walked through the front door. Why do you suppose the culprit did otherwise?"

"I don't know, sir. Maybe he thought the door was locked."

"Hmm! So how would the murderer have entered the house if the doors were locked and the window catch seized?" Again, he left them thinking before continuing.

"Constable, if you'd broken the pane to escape, how long would it have taken you to climb through, without catching your clothing on the broken glass and avoiding cutting yourself?"

"A minute or more, sir."

"How come then, you heard the glass break, then a moment later saw the suspect run out of the mews?"

PC Richards thought for a while. "Perhaps he was particularly agile, sir, and dived through the window, straight into a forward roll, jumping back onto his feet then away at a sprint?"

"If well-practised at such manoeuvres, that *would* be possible. Let me suggest another scenario. You, Richards, were in the house with Finchley. You slipped into the kitchen, took a knife from the block, then carried it surreptitiously into the sitting room and awaited your opportunity. When Finchley turned away, you grabbed him from behind and used the knife to sever his windpipe and carotid artery. His legs flayed around, knocking over the chair and table. His hand flew into the air to reach back, hitting the chandelier. But he could not reach you and, in any case... it was all over quickly, his life extinguished. He collapsed onto the ground."

This suggestion dumfounded Richards. Locke-Croft went on, continuing to stare directly at the constable: "After the deed, you took the Oddfellows badge from Finchley's coat and dropped it onto the floor, so it would be found later – not overlooked. You left the house by the door, walked down the street, and deposited the knife into a drain, before quickly returning to the property. Then Richards, you waited until a man came trotting past, smashed the window from the outside, blew your whistle and shouted stop. In fear of being framed for a crime he'd not committed he ran off and you gave chase. But after the fugitive entered the park, you ceased chasing him and returned to the scene to offer your assistance."

The others in the room looked at Richards, astounded.

"Moreover, in your report you stated that the man had disappeared in the park's wooded section. I've been to that part of Regent's Park and the trees provide no hiding places. They are sparsely planted with few low-level branches and leaves. A four-year-old, playing *hide and seek* could have found the accused, if he'd wanted to. But you didn't want to catch him at all, did you Richards?"

Now Richards rose. "What reason could *I* have had to kill this man? I'd never met him. I'd no motive."

"Or so you would have us believe, constable. In fact, you do know James Finchley. It is on record that you were a client of Chippenham and Dudley Solicitors, of Weymouth Street. Do you deny it?"

"No, sir, I cannot refute that, but my appointment was with Mr Chippenham himself."

"Indeed, it was, constable. The appointments book at that firm corroborates this. At the time you arrived, however, Mr Chippenham was otherwise disposed, and you and your wife were shown into the offices of James Finchley, instead. So, you just lied to us Richards."

Richards responded speedily "We *were* seen by another solicitor, but I never learned his name. I didn't know the person on the floor at No 7 Park Square Mews was that same man until you told me."

Locke-Croft let Richards stew for a minute before resuming his attack. "Your wife is a beautiful young woman, would you not say, Richards?"

"She most certainly is."

"A beauty so great that any red-blooded fellow would want to bed her!"

"How dare you speak about my wife like this?"

"It would be natural then for you to wish to take revenge on any man that tried to force himself upon her, wouldn't it, Richards?" Richards sat again silently, his expression showing his exasperation.

"Looking further at Chippenham and Dudley records, I noted that a second appointment was made at the offices, at an hour when you were on the beat and unable to attend. Your wife attended the solicitors' chambers alone. I put it to you that whilst alone with Finchley, he tried to seduce her and touched her inappropriately. She reported this to you, but knowing it was only her word against his, you planned retribution on the man."

This time, it was the Superintendent who stood. "This is ridiculous." He turned toward the Chief Constable. "With all due respect, sir, you appear to have employed an idiot. This so-called consulting detective first accused DI Harrison of the crime, then the good Doctor Williams, before turning his accusations to PC Richards. Who is to be *next*, I ask?" Bateman sat down again, his face stern, and the Chief started to rise.

"Sir, please allow me to continue. All will become clear within minutes. What I just demonstrated is there are three people *within this room* who had the opportunity, means and motive to carry out this murder. If you will permit me, I *shall* expose the murderer."

The Chief Constable's legs relaxed, and he returned to a sitting position, resigned that they must listen a little longer. "Gentlemen, I know this has been a challenging time for those accused but please be patient. We shall give Locke-Croft a few more minutes."

"Richards. I am told that you assisted Detective Goldsworthy with door-to-door enquiries along Brunswick Place. Correct?"

"Yes, sir. It was on my beat, so I knocked on a few doors to help him."

"I further understand that Goldsworthy found one person on his side of the street who had seen the suspect, and she had directed him to Camden Market. But you reported that none of the people you spoke to had noticed anything." Richards nodded to confirm this.

"But I called on those same houses and three people reported they had noticed a man running from a policeman." Locke-Croft stared into the PC's eyes. "Conceivably, Richards, you had reason *not* to identify the fugitive. Or perhaps you are just incompetent?"

Goldsworthy looked disbelievingly at Richards, wondering why his friend Ernest had drawn a blank in Brunswick Place, when there *had* been witnesses. Others in the room eyed Richards suspiciously. DCI Weatherspoon wondered whether he had been right to recommend him for a move into the detective branch.

Locke-Croft strode around, thinking things through, before addressing the gathering again. "When Richards returned to Park Square Mews, twenty minutes after leaving the area, he found DI Harrison directing officers, yet Scotland Yard is a good thirty-minute walk from the mews. Strange that he was already in attendance."

Harrison went to speak, but Locke-Croft turned towards the doctor. "Mr Williams," he said, purposely not addressing him by his deserved title, to antagonise him, "You were on the crime scene within thirty minutes of the murder, even though your department is in Westminster, an hour's walk to reach the scene. Care to enlighten us how you came to be at Park Square Mews so promptly?"

The doctor's expression gave away his annoyance. His brow was creased, his eyebrows almost touching, and his eyes stared at the detective. "Have you not heard of the Underground Railways of London? Walking is not the only way to move about our great capital."

"Ah! The Underground. Which route did you take that day?"

"Well," the doctor paused, looking flustered. "Err, I would have taken the District Line to Charring Cross, then the Bakerloo Line onward to Regent's Park station."

"Hmm. How did you come to hear your presence was needed?"

"I received a telephone call."

"At what hour was this?"

"I can't remember the exact time."

"And who was it that phoned you?"

"I don't recall the name of the officer. *Someone* at the Yard."

"I checked the records, Dr Williams. No one at Scotland Yard made a call. So how come you knew about this murder and arrived at the scene just ten minutes after the detective inspector. Was it perhaps telepathic instead of telephonic? Coincidences, coincidences, coincidences. *Too* many coincidences, gentlemen.

"For the doctor to have been at the crime scene within thirty minutes of the murder being discovered, he must have known it had occurred before he could have been informed. Yet the evidence is that no one advised him. If someone had seen Williams nearby and apprised him of the homicide, this timescale could be met. But he has just told us he received a phone call and travelled by the Underground... How could this be?"

"Moreover, I contacted the headquarters of Underground Railways and enquired about trains when Williams would have us believe he was travelling. There were *none*, gentlemen. There had been a suicide on the Bakerloo Line, and all trains were inactive between Charring Cross and Regent's Park."

He paced back and forth again, with all eyes following him.

"Gentlemen. It is evident that Harrison did not adequately investigate the death of James Finchley. Yet he has an excellent reputation for thoroughness. The doctor arrived at the scene impossibly early, with no one telling him about the crime, and PC Richards appears to have avoided catching the suspect he chased. Each of these officers may have motives for seeking revenge. All three had the means and opportunity to conduct this killing. But *who* is the murderer?"

"What none of these men know is that I possess the missing knife from Finchley's kitchen and forensics lifted a partial fingerprint from its hilt."

Again, he watched the body language of the three suspects. "I also have the print of a fingertip, used to draw the dust circles on Finchley's sideboard. I know that the assailant was taller than his victim and favoured his left hand."

"Two of the officers identified as having means, opportunity and perhaps motive are left-handed."

PC Richards relaxed into his chair, knowing he was off the hook. The other two sat rigidly, as DC Smith entered the room and passed documents to Locke-Croft, who scanned the papers before continuing.

"Gentlemen. Before I called you into this place, I despatched

Constable Smith with a task that he has now completed. He has acquired written evidence confirming my suspicions about the motive for this crime. I can now reveal that the murderer is." He paused for effect. "Doctor Williams."

Williams jumped up as if to protest, then looked toward the door, wondering whether an escape was possible. The Chief Constable stood and asked. "Locke-Croft, my dear chap, please share with us what evidence you have that proves Doctor Williams killed Finchley."

"Of course. The first point that supports my supposition is that the neighbour opposite Finchley's house reported that on the morning of the murder, a woman matching the description of Mrs Williams was seen leaving his house. Additionally, hairs taken from a brush in Finchley's bedroom — he held up the evidence bag containing them — show that this woman had stayed in that room."

He looked directly at Williams, noting his stern face but with a hint of resignation. "Doctor, you did not document in your report that the fatal incision had been made by a left-handed taller killer. You are left-handed and taller than the victim. Furthermore, you suggested a kitchen knife was the likely weapon used to cut Finchley's throat, and one was missing from Finchley's kitchen. When I examined the body, however, I discovered that an extremely sharp, fine blade must have been used. A cook's knife could not have created the cut, especially one as blunt as that pulled from the drains just up from the murder scene." He emphasised the point by holding up the knife again in its evidence pouch.

"Moreover," he turned and lifted another evidence bag from his case, containing a scalpel, "this instrument has been examined and has on it traces that match with James Finchley's blood.

This scalpel, Gentlemen, had *not* been used during the autopsy on the victim. All those tools had been cleaned or disposed of by the mortuary assistant. This one was found in a bin... at the doctor's residence."

There was movement in the room, as the facts were revealed, and Locke-Croft noticed the Chief Constable about to speak.

"I have not yet finished. Mrs Williams has confirmed her affair with James Finchley and verified my supposition that she was planning to leave her husband, thus proving my motive theory. In addition, the distance between toe and heel tips of the doctor's shoes match the scratches made by the murderer, in Finchley's sitting-room floorboards."

Williams looked at his shoes. "Not those shoes, Doctor. The pair that were in your cloakroom at home. Your wife is in a room along the corridor from here. Shall I call her in now to confront you? It's time you came clean, sir."

Smith moved closer to the pathologist, ready to apprehend him.

"Damn you, Locke-Croft. Yes, I killed Finchley. The man was a bounder. You were correct. He had seduced Agatha, and she was planning to abandon me. I went to plead with him – an Oddfellow member and one who I would have expected brotherhood, not betrayal. But his commitment to the cause of friendship and mutual support did not extend to anyone other than himself. He refused to leave my wife alone, and he said she would be joining him that very day. I lost my temper and disposed of Finchley with one stroke."

The Chief Constable stood. "Harrison, arrest Doctor Williams."

"Not so fast, sir. I am not yet done. There is still the matter of Harrison's apparent incompetence. His lacklustre investigation that should have already exposed the Doctor as the murderer."

Locke-Croft waited as this additional accusation sunk into the minds of those present.

"You may as well come clean, Harrison. Your prints are on the knife and the supposed candelabra circles that you made when attempting to provide an alternative motive for the murder – one that would help your friend Doctor Williams to escape justice."

"No. no. It's not true. I had no hand in covering up the doctor's crime. Call me incompetent if you must, but don't accuse me of colluding with the murderer."

"Perhaps your claim to be incompetent would be reasonable, had you not created the sideboard dust rings? Maybe distraction was a reasonable excuse, as your mind was on other things. But the distraction would be that your wife, too, had fallen for Finchley's charms. Had the doctor not got to him first, you would undoubtedly have disposed of the man yourself."

"I dispute everything you say, Locke-Croft, and you cannot prove any of your suppositions."

"I have here your wife's statement, confirming her affair with James Finchley. This was your motive, Harrison. It was you who made the rings in the dust. It was you who broke the window and pretended the latch to be jammed. And it was you who, out of character, failed to investigate the crime thoroughly... You cannot deny this."

Harrison looked at his fellow officers then back to Locke-Croft, his expression giving away his shame, defeated by the evidence. "Yes," he loudly declared. "The damned man was a scoundrel. I had welcomed him into our home for dinner, where he'd met my wife. Then the bastard pursued her, wooed her with expensive presents and seduced her while I was hard at work tracking down

London's criminals." Harrison was fuming, his face flushed with blood as he unloaded his guilt.

"I visited his house to warn him off, not to murder him. As I arrived at his door, there came the sound of a commotion and a crash, so I entered the property and found Doctor Williams at his side, a scalpel in his hand."

Locke-Croft smirked at this revelation. Harrison had provided even stronger evidence for Williams' conviction.

The Chief Constable was flabbergasted. "Superintendent. Get Harrison's statement and charge him with perverting the course of justice and accessory to murder. I want the report on my desk in the morning... Silvester, please come with me."

The law officers were astonished at the news that one of their colleagues had been the murderer and another assisted him with trying to evade justice. Never again would they assume innocence amongst their own.

* * *

"What I'd like to know, Silvester, is why you accused PC Richards of the murder, as well as Williams and Harrison, if you knew he hadn't committed the crime. Why all the theatricals and slanderous accusations?"

"My dear Chief Constable. I had worked out who was responsible for Finchley's death and who had aided the murderer, but I needed to build the drama leading to confessions. Richards was guilty of merely trying to cover up his poor fitness and lack of determination, and of his incompetence in the detective role. But swinging the accusations amongst the *three* suspects achieved my purpose."

Locke-Croft went on. "If the evidence had been offered

undramatically, their minds would have been unencumbered and thinking more clearly. The drama led to tension, the worry of being exposed to stress, and when faced with what appeared to be irrefutable evidence, to their confessions. Without their admitting the crimes, it would have proven much more difficult for you to gain convictions."

"Although Harrison might also have been goaded into attacking Mr James – privileged, arrogant – Finchley, it was Williams who did the deed. The man probably deserved to die. He was a predator and a parasite. But where would society be if we all took justice into our own hands?"

"Silvester. There are one or two things I'd like you to clarify for me. If the doctor carried out the murder, why was his cuff not blooded?"

"It is my belief that Harrison sent him away to get cleaned up and when he returned, he was wearing rubber gloves that covered his cuffs, so none of the other officers could see the bloodstains."

"Hmm... You mentioned Harrison's ill-fitting overcoat and another coat with a blooded sleeve. Please explain these."

"When Harrison altered the crime scene to make it look like a fight had taken place, he must have moved the body and his sleeve become bloodied. Since he was to take control of the investigation, the opportunity to clean his sleeve of blood was not available, so he swapped his coat for Finchley's, which was a size smaller. It was Richards who noticed the anomaly. Harrison's story about accidentally taking his brother-in-law's coat will prove to be a lie, I'm sure."

Locke-Croft handed the Chief Constable a large package. "You will require these documents and physical evidence that I gathered during my investigation. I'll leave it with you and your officers to conclude the case. I remain at your call when you are again in need of my services. Good day to you, Charles."

He turned on his heels and strode out of the office and station...

* * *

The Solution - Afterword

Dear Relative, having now read the story's concluding part, you must already have judged correctly who murdered Finchley and which other person had tried to cover up the crime. You did not have the luxury of manipulating the gathered suspects to prompt confessions. You will, nonetheless, have drawn the same conclusions and provided your reasoning to the satisfaction of my representatives. I congratulate you.

* * *

The Long Wait

Hicks finished reading the Solution and placed it back into its envelope, then sat in contemplation. Discovering the culprit had astounded him. He'd thought Harrison as the most likely suspect, but he'd never foreseen the outcome. His client must have the brainpower of a chess master to unravel the evidence and reach the conclusion. Whoever passed this test would deserve the inheritance. He suspected that there might be many generations of relatives who would fail, and he may well have died by the time this happened.

Hicks returned to his office, gave the Test and his client's letter to his ever-on-duty secretary for filing and placed the Solution into his safe. It would remain there until the death of his client.

* * *

Acknowledgements

This is my second book, and I couldn't have done it without lots of assistance. I'd like to thank the following people who provided feedback on earlier drafts (in no particular order): Monica Bennett, Keith Salmon, Pete Bennett, Anastasia Woodcock, Julie Bosworth, and Annette Salmon. A special mention must also be made of Jamie Salmon, for the great cover design. Thank you all.

More?

If you would like to know more about the next Suzanna McLeod episode, *The Duty*, check out my website: www.harrynavinski.com/.

The Duty is the second book in the DCI Suzanna McLeod series. In it, you'll hear more about her taking the Test and how it changed her life. If you like fast-paced, inspired criminal investigations and the thrill of the chase, you'll love Harry Navinski's new novel.

About the Author

From Hercules to Handlooms, then Harry Navinski.

During his 3+ decades of aircraft engineering in the Royal Air Force – first as a technician, then an engineering officer – Harry created and edited the RAF's sports and adventurous activities magazine, RAF Active.

After his RAF days, Harry spent time on voluntary service in India, setting up a programme, obtaining funds and establishing manufacturing units to provide work for women who had been forced into the sex trade or were at high risk of being trafficked.

His last RAF job was managing a Hercules engineering support squadron, and the role in India was primarily managing a wooden-framed hand-loom factory - a world apart in technology.

He wrote his first novel, *The Glass*, after returning from India.

This set him on a new career path, as a crime fiction author.

You can connect with me on:

🌐 https://www.harrynavinski.com

🐦 https://twitter.com/HarryNavinski

📘 https://www.facebook.com/harry.navinski9

🔗 https://www.goodreads.com/author/show/20525174.Harry_Navinski

🔗 https://www.amazon.co.uk/Harry-Navinski/e/B08DJDB7FM?ref=sr_ntt_srch_lnk_1&qid=1620489058&sr=8-1

Also by Harry Navinski

My writing style is influenced by some of the best British TV crime series, such as Vera, Morse, Lewis, Endeavour, Broadchurch and New Tricks. They're full of dialogue and action, rather than lengthy descriptions. They start with the crime and finish when the criminals have been charged. Along the way, there are dead ends and challenges: physical, mental and emotional. I hope you enjoy them.

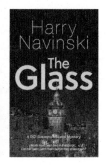

The Glass
First in the DCI Suzanna McLeod mystery series. Suzanna's Edinburgh-based team has a reputation to live up to. But the Chief Superintendent is a by-the-book meddler and her team have personal problems that need her help.

Under pressure to catch armed robbers before they strike again, Suzanna's focus is challenged when her inherited magnifying glass is stolen – a cherished item that led to her becoming a detective. The young thief could never have known the impact its theft would have on him and his family.

As the chase is underway for the gunmen, Suzanna takes on the most dangerous of the criminals. But even after the case appears to be drawing to a close, something is nagging at Suzanna's gut. What could they have missed?

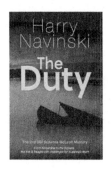

The Duty

From Kincardine to Kolkata, Suzanna is determined to find the killer of a young woman found mutilated and drowned, as well as track down the man who knifed her own team member, DI Una Wallace. Illegal immigration, slavery, and brutality surface as she closes in.

Suzanna's up against her own Chief Superintendent's nit-picking interference, plus Kolkata's uncooperative police force and the violent gangsters who force poor women into sexual slavery, while navigating her own love-life dilemma.

Threats, fights, chases, and undercover work ensue before she gains what she needs from tropical Bengal and returns to chilly Scotland to seek the evidence for convictions.

The Duty is an incredible, challenging, emotional journey, from start to finish.

Printed in Great Britain
by Amazon